"Are you sure I can't pay you for tutoring Jane?"

"No. We've been through this before, Samuel. I don't want your money. I'm doing this for your daughter."

"Then at least let me take you out for dinner."

"I don't—"

"Please, Beth. I feel like I should do something for you."

She paused on the porch, looking back at Samuel framed in the doorway with the light behind him and his features in the shadows. Dinner? Like a real date? The more she found out about Samuel, the more she liked him—and he didn't fit into her future plans at all, especially with his ready-made family.

MARGARET DALEY

feels she has been blessed. She has been married thirty-three years to her husband, Mike, whom she met in college. He is a terrific support and her best friend. They have one son, Shaun, who married his high school sweetheart in June 2002.

Margaret has been writing for many years and loves to tell a story. When she was a little girl, she would play with her dolls and make up stories about their lives. Now she writes these stories down. She especially enjoys weaving stories about families and how faith in God can sustain a person when things get tough. When she isn't writing, she is fortunate to be a teacher for students with special needs. Margaret has taught for over twenty years and loves working with her students. She has also been a Special Olympics coach and has participated in many sports with her students.

LIGHT IN THE STORM

MARGARET DALEY

Steeple Hill®

Published by Steeple Hill Books™

STEEPLE HILL BOOKS

Steeple
Hill®

ISBN 0-373-81211-6

LIGHT IN THE STORM

www.SteepleHill.com

Printed in U.S.A.

With us is the Lord our God
to help us and to fight our battles.
—*2 Chronicles* 32:8

To my readers—I appreciate your support.

To my local RWA chapter, Romance Writers Ink—
You are a wonderful group of writers.

Chapter One

With a huff Jane Morgan plopped into her desk. "I don't see why I have to be here."

Beth Coleman sighed, turned from watching the snow falling outside Sweetwater High School and said, "Because you'll be the topic of conversation. It's your future we'll be discussing. I thought you should have a say in it."

Flipping her long, dark brown hair behind her shoulders, Jane slouched in her desk, her arms folded over her chest, a pout firmly in place. "What future? Don't you get it? I don't want to be here."

Beth again looked at the snow coming down and wondered if this was the best time to have a parent conference. Of course, when she had contacted Jane's father yesterday, there hadn't been any snow. "Does your father have a cell phone?" Maybe she should call him and cancel until the weather was better. She could drive Jane home.

"Yes."

As with Jane's performance in class the past few weeks since the teenager had enrolled at the beginning of the second semester, Beth realized she would have to ask what the number was, because Jane wouldn't give any information unless she absolutely had to. "What is—"

"Sorry I'm late, but as you can see, the weather is getting bad." A large man with blond hair and brown eyes stood framed in the classroom doorway.

Speechless for a few seconds, Beth just stared at Jane's father. Samuel Morgan wasn't anything like her image of him when she'd talked to him briefly the day before. His voice was gruff and deep, but his looks were refined—handsome but not ruggedly so. More along the lines of a male model she'd seen in a magazine selling cologne. Whoa! Why in the world had she thought that?

Beth mentally shook her head and crossed the room. Presenting her hand, which he took in a firm grip and shook, she said, "I'm Jane's English teacher, Beth Coleman. Please come in and have a seat—unless you'd rather reschedule this meeting because of the snow. It doesn't look like it's going to let up any time soon."

He shrugged out of his heavy black wool overcoat, ran a hand through his wet, conservatively cut hair and entered the room. "No, this is too important to postpone. And besides, I'm here, so we might as well talk now. Don't you agree, Jane?"

When Samuel squeezed into the desk next to his daughter, Beth noticed how he dwarfed it, even though it was standard size for a high school class. She knew he was a minister, and yet for a brief moment he seemed more a warrior than a peacemaker.

"Sure. Why not?" Jane averted her face, staring off into space, defiance in every line of her body.

"On the phone, Miss Coleman, you said that Jane was having a problem with the work you've assigned."

Beth took a desk near the pair, scooting it around so she faced both of them. "She isn't doing any of the work. She's been here nearly two weeks and I have yet to see anything from her. We've had four graded assignments so far this semester. She has a zero right now."

"Not one grade?" Samuel asked Jane, his tension conveyed by his clenched jaw and frown.

His daughter lifted her shoulders in a shrug, but didn't say a word, her head remaining turned away.

"Is there a problem I'm not aware of?" Beth saw a flash of vulnerability appear in his dark eyes before he masked the expression. It touched a part of her that over the years had seen many single parents struggle to do the job of both mother and father.

"As I'm sure you're aware, we've just moved here." He glanced at his daughter. "Jane has never adjusted well to new towns."

"How many times have you moved?"

"This is our sixth move. I was a chaplain in the army until recently. We're both looking forward to settling down in one place."

"Adjusting to a new town can be tough. If Jane's willing to work and stay after school to make up the assignments, I'll take them late this time."

"What do you say, Jane?" Samuel leaned forward, his hands laced together on top of the desk. His whitened knuckles indicated nothing casual in the gesture.

His daughter, silent, peered at the snow falling, as though she hadn't heard the question.

"Jane?" A firmness entered his deep, gruff voice.

She swung her gaze to her father, her pout deepening. Chewing on her bottom lip, she stared at him, several emotions vying for dominance. Anger won out over a need to please.

"Would you rather the zeros remain on your grade?" he asked with an underlying calm that amazed Beth.

Samuel Morgan was the new reverend of Sweetwater Community Church, where she attended. It was obvious that he had a great deal of patience, if his dealings with his daughter were any indication. That was comforting to know, since Reverend Collins, their previous minister, had been beloved by all in the congregation.

Jane sighed, straightening in the desk. "If you must know, I didn't understand a couple of the assign-ments."

"Did you ask Miss Coleman for help?"

"No."

"Jane, I'll be glad to help you when you stay to complete the work. And for that matter, any other assignment you have trouble with. All you have to do is ask me for help. That's part of my job."

The teenager looked at Beth as if she thought Beth was crazy to think she was going to ask for any assistance on an assignment, especially in a class of thirty students. Beth wondered if something else was going on beneath Jane's defiance. It wasn't that unusual to see a teen rebel, but Beth sensed a troubled soul begging for help. She made a mental note to check with the young woman to see if she understood her homework assignments. Sometimes when a student moved a lot, she lost ground because curriculum wasn't always the same in each school.

"Miss Coleman, Jane will stay after school every day until she has made up her work. Since I pick her up, it shouldn't be a problem."

Beth slipped from the desk. "We can start Monday. Hopefully the weather will be clear by then."

Samuel rose. "She'll be here."

Jane shoved herself out of the desk, pushing it several inches across the hardwood floor. "Maybe we're in for a blizzard."

"We don't often have blizzards in Sweetwater," Beth said with a smile. Even as a teacher she enjoyed the occasional snow day when school was canceled.

"That's good to hear, because it sure is snowing hard now," Samuel said, looking toward the window.

"Now, that's something to pray about," Jane mumbled, starting for the door.

Samuel watched his daughter leave the classroom. "Sorry about that, Miss Coleman."

"Please call me Beth. I haven't had a chance to tell you, but I attend Sweetwater Community Church."

His brows rose. "You do? I didn't see you there last week."

"I'm sorry I missed your first Sunday, but I was taking my brother to college in Louisville. He just started this semester and he had to move into the dorm."

"Then I look forward to seeing you this Sunday." His gaze again slid to the window. "That is, if we don't have that blizzard my daughter is praying for."

Beth fitted her hand in his to shake goodbye and was conscious of something else beside its firmness—a warmth. A warmth that shot up her arm and made her very aware of the man before her. The warrior impression she'd received earlier was tempered with the calmness he'd exhibited when dealing with his daughter. He gave off mixed messages, which intrigued Beth. She suspected he was more adept at listening to other people's problems than telling anyone his.

"Tomorrow the sun will be shining. Mark my words, Reverend Morgan."

"Hope you're right, Miss—Beth. And please call me Samuel." He walked toward the door, turned back and added, "I still have a lot to do to finish moving in and bad weather definitely puts a damper on things."

Before she realized what she was really doing, Beth asked, "Can I help with anything?" The second the words were out of her mouth, she bit down on her lower lip. Her first weekend in years without any obligations, and she was volunteering to help the reverend put his house in order. When would she learn? She didn't have to be there for everyone. It was okay to take some time for herself.

He chuckled. "Thanks for the offer, but I know how many papers English teachers have to grade. My children and I will get it done…if not this weekend, then the next."

When he left, Beth walked to the window and stared at the swirling mass of white, watching for Jane and Samuel to come out the front door. When they emerged, they were quickly obscured by the blowing snow. She loved cold weather and the occasional snow they had in Sweetwater. It brought out the child she'd never been allowed to be. But this storm might be worse than she had originally thought.

Beth headed for her desk and quickly gathered those papers that the reverend had mentioned, stuffing them into her briefcase to grade over the weekend. But she promised herself as she left her classroom that she would find some time to make a snowman and give him a carrot for his nose and pieces of bark for his eyes and mouth.

After pulling her cap down over her ears and tying her wool scarf around her neck, Beth exited the school building and walked toward where she knew she had parked her white car, even though in the driving snow it wasn't visible. Halfway to the parking lot she spied her Jeep and quickened her steps. Out of the corner of her eye she saw a blue

Ford Mustang with the reverend and Jane standing next to it.

Why haven't they left? Beth wondered, and changed her destination.

"Something wrong?" she asked as she approached the pair arguing while the snow blew around them.

Samuel stopped what he was going to say to his daughter and glanced toward Beth. "I was for going back inside and getting help. Jane was for hiking home." He gestured toward his car. "Won't start."

"You probably can't get anyone out here to help right now. Every tow truck will be busy just trying to haul people out of ditches. I can give you a ride home and you can see what's wrong with your car tomorrow—if this snow lets up."

"You're not going to get an argument out of me. Where are you parked?"

Beth waved her hand toward her five-year-old Jeep Cherokee. "I don't usually have too much trouble in the snow."

As they trudged toward the Jeep, Jane mumbled something under her breath. If her tight-lipped expression was any hint, Beth was glad she hadn't heard what the teenager had said. When Beth reached her car, she unlocked her doors and slid inside while Jane plopped herself in the back seat and Samuel climbed into the front.

"You're staying at the rectory, aren't you?" Beth asked, starting the engine.

"Yes. I hope it isn't too far out of your way."

"Practically on my way home."

Samuel stared out the windshield. "Can I help you scrape the windows clear of snow? I'm not sure how much good it will do, as fast as the snow is coming down."

Turning a knob on the dashboard, Beth cranked up the heat. "Let me warm up the car first, then we'll see what can be done about the windows." She peered over her shoulder. "Jane, I've got two scrapers under the front seat. Can you reach them for me?"

With her mouth slashing downward, Jane produced the two scrapers and thrust them at Beth.

"In fact, since we're inconveniencing you, Jane and I will take care of the windows while you stay warm in here," Samuel offered.

"Dad," Jane protested.

"Yes? Do you have a problem with that? You can always walk like you wanted to a few minutes ago."

Jane folded her arms across her chest, her hands clenched, and stared out the side, muttering under her breath.

Beth started to decline the offer of help, but she caught Samuel's look. He shook his head as though he knew what she was going to say and wanted her to accept their assistance. She snapped her mouth closed and gave him the scrapers.

While Samuel and Jane cleared the snow and ice built up on the windows, Beth watched, feeling guilty that she was warm while they were freezing. She didn't accept help well and this was making her very uncomfortable, especially when she saw Jane's face set in a frown, her cheeks red from the cold, her body beginning to shake because she was dressed in a short skirt with a heavy jacket that covered her only to her waist. Except for a pair of half boots, large portions of the teenager's legs were exposed to the fierce elements. At least she wore gloves, Beth thought, tapping her hand against the steering wheel to keep herself from snatching the scraper from Jane and finishing the job.

Ten minutes later father and daughter settled back into the Jeep, their sighs indicating they relished the warmth. Beth's guilt soared.

She had a problem with wanting to do everything for everyone else. She had to learn to say no and to let others do for her. Darcy and Jesse were always telling her that at their Saturday get-togethers. She should listen to her friends. But it was tough to go against ingrained behavior.

Negotiating out of the parking lot, Beth drove slowly, glad that most people were off the roads and hopefully safely in their homes. "Too much longer and I'm afraid we would have been stuck at school."

Jane gave a choking sound, which caused her father to send a censuring look her way. Having raised three siblings as well as teaching high schoolers for the past fifteen years, Beth understood the inner workings of a teenage mind. Jane fitted into the category of those who hated school and would rather be anywhere but there—hence her desire to strike out and walk home in a snowstorm, even though she wasn't dressed properly for any kind of walk.

"Where were you last stationed in the army?" Beth asked, hating the silence that had descended.

With his gaze fixed on the road ahead, Samuel said, "Leavenworth."

"Where the prison is?"

"Yes."

"Stuck in the middle of nowhere," Jane offered from the back seat.

"Were you ever stationed overseas?"

"Germany and Japan, which gave us a chance to see that part of the world."

Thinking of all the places she would love to visit, Beth chanced a quick look toward Samuel. "That must have been interesting."

"If you could speak the language," Jane said.

Beth heard the pout in the teenager's voice, but didn't turn to look at her. She could imagine the crossed arms and defiant expression on the girl's face, often a permanent part of her countenance. "True. That could be a problem, but they have such wonderful programs for teaching languages. I've been using a taped series to learn Spanish."

"I always tried to learn at least some of the language when we were stationed in a country. Japanese was hard, but I found German easy, especially to read." Samuel shifted in his seat, taking his attention from the road. With a smile he asked, "Have you traveled much?"

Beth shook her head. "But that's about to

change. My brother's at college, so as of a week ago I have no one left at home." Beth recalled the mixed emotions she had experienced when she had said goodbye to Daniel at school. Elation at the sense of freedom she now had mingled with sadness that he would be starting a part of his life without her.

"Are you planning on going somewhere they speak Spanish?"

"Yes, but I don't know where yet. I'm going to spread a map of Central and South America out in front of me and throw a dart. I'm going where it lands."

Samuel chuckled. "An unusual method of planning a vacation."

"It won't be a vacation. I want to live there, for a while at least."

"What about Brazil? That takes up a good portion of South America, and they speak Portuguese."

"I understand there are a lot of similarities between the two languages. If I end up in Brazil, it will just make the adventure even more exciting."

"So when are you going to throw that dart?"

"Soon. I'm thinking of having a party and

inviting all my friends to be there for the big moment." Saying out loud what she had been toying with for the past few months made her firm the decision to have a party in celebration of a new phase in her life, even though she rarely threw parties.

Beth pulled up in front of the rectory, a large two-story white Victorian house that sat next to the Sweetwater Community Church. "Tomorrow call Al's Body Shop. He should be able to help you with your car. He's a member of the church."

Jane threw open the back door and jumped out, hurrying toward the front door, her uncomfortable-looking high-heeled short boots sinking beneath the blanket of snow.

Samuel observed his daughter for a few seconds, then turned to Beth. "Thanks for the ride. You're a lifesaver. Are you sure you'll be okay going home alone?"

"I'll be fine. I only live three blocks over. If it gets too bad, I can always walk and then call Al's tomorrow myself."

"At least you're more suitably dressed for a hike in the snow than my daughter. I'd better let you go." He opened the door. "I'll have a talk with Jane, and she'll be there after school on Monday."

As he climbed from the Jeep, Beth said, "See you Sunday."

Samuel plodded toward the porch while Beth inched her car away from the curb. He was thankful she had been there to help them with a ride home. Just from the short time he had been around the woman he got the impression she went out of her way to assist people when she could. He liked that about her.

Picturing Beth in his mind, he smiled. Her blue eyes had sparkled with kindness and her generous mouth had curved with a smile meant to put a person at ease. He imagined she had a hard time keeping her reddish-brown hair tamed and in control, but he liked it, because every other aspect of Miss Beth Coleman was restrained, down to her neat gray dress and matching pumps. She probably thought of her long curly hair as her bane, while he thought it softened her prim and proper facade.

Taking one last look back, Samuel noticed the white Jeep quickly disappearing in the blowing snow. The bad weather had swept through so quickly that it had caught most people off guard. The only good thing about today was that Aunt Mae had arrived before the storm.

When he entered his house, where boxes were still stacked all over the place, delicious aromas teased him, causing his stomach to rumble. At least now with Aunt Mae here, they would have a decent meal instead of his feeble attempts at cooking. There was even a chance that his house would come together before summer vacation.

Shaking off the snow that still clung to him, he stomped his feet on the mat he was sure Aunt Mae had placed in front of the door, then shrugged out of his overcoat. He took a deep breath, trying to figure out what his aunt was preparing for dinner. Onions. Garlic. Meat. Hoping it was her spaghetti, he headed toward the kitchen to see.

"Dad."

Samuel stopped in the doorway into the den and peered over the mound of boxes to find his middle child on the floor with his bottom stuck up in the air while he tried to look under the couch. "Did you lose something, Craig?"

His son straightened, one hand clutched around his Game Boy. "Allie is hiding things again. Can't you do something about her?"

"I'll have a talk with her. How's your room coming along?" Samuel asked, realizing his son must have gotten some of his things put away or the Game Boy wouldn't be in his hand.

Craig hopped to his feet. "I'm through."

"Good, son." Samuel moved toward the kitchen, making a note to himself to check Craig's room. His son's version of clean was definitely not his.

In the kitchen Samuel found his aunt by the stove adding something to a big pot while his youngest stood on a chair next to her and stirred whatever was cooking in the big pan. "Smells wonderful. Spaghetti?"

Aunt Mae glanced over her shoulder. "Yes. That's what Allie and Craig wanted. They said something about being tired of peanut butter and jelly sandwiches."

"You know how hopeless I am in the kitchen."

She tsked. "Samuel, after over two years you'd think I would have rubbed off on you."

"Aunt Mae, don't ever go away again," Allie said in a serious voice while continuing to stir the sauce.

His aunt, a woman who obviously loved her own cooking, tousled Allie's hair. "Hopefully my sister won't hurt herself again. I didn't like being away from you all."

"Next time Aunt Kathy can come here instead of you going there." Allie laid the spoon on the counter.

Visions of Mae's older sister living with them sent panic through Samuel. He started to say something about his eight-year-old daughter's suggestion.

Aunt Mae's blue eyes twinkled and two dimples appeared in her cheeks. "Oh, sugar, that probably wouldn't be too good of an idea. She's *very* set in her ways. Besides, she was bedridden for a week and couldn't travel."

"Well, we missed you." Allie threw her arms around Aunt Mae.

The older woman brushed back the few strands of gray hair that had come loose from her bun, fighting tears that had suddenly filled her eyes. "I missed you all."

"Is that coffee on the stove?" Samuel asked, feeling his own emotions close to the surface—which he attributed to his exhaustion. He walked to the counter where some cups were set out and retrieved one.

As Samuel poured his coffee, he corralled his emotions and shoved them to the dark recesses of his mind. Aunt Mae had been a lifesaver after his wife died. When she had arrived on his doorstep, their lives had been in total chaos. Ruth's death had hit him so hard that it had taken him months to see how much his children needed him. Thankfully Aunt Mae had been around to ease their sorrow, because he hadn't been able to—something he still felt guilty about.

"Was everything all right at school with Jane?" Aunt Mae asked, opening the refrigerator and taking out the ingredients for a salad.

"Allie!" Craig's voice echoed through the house.

His youngest daughter jumped down from the chair, scooted it back toward the table, then darted out of the kitchen.

"No doubt she hid more than Craig's Game Boy." Samuel shook his head as he heard footsteps pounding up the stairs. "Jane's having trouble in English. I'm going to check on Monday to see how she's doing in her other classes." He took a long sip of his coffee, relishing the hot drink after being out in the cold.

"She took her mother's death harder than the other two."

"She was really close to Ruth." He drank some more to ease the constriction in his throat.

"Still, something else might be going on with her, Samuel. A good prayer might help."

There was a time he had felt that way. Now he didn't know if that would help his daughter. He kissed his aunt on the cheek. "You have good intuition. I'll keep an eye on her." Shouts from above drew Samuel's attention. "I'd better go and referee those two."

"Dinner will be ready in an hour."

Samuel strode toward the stairs. He was the new minister of Sweetwater Community Church and he wasn't even sure how effective prayer was. His house was still in chaos. He longed for the time he'd felt confident in the power of the Lord—before He had taken his wife and thrown his family into turmoil. He shouldn't have taken this church assignment, but he was desperate. He wanted his old life back.

Beth took a paper cup filled with red fruit punch from the table next to the coffee urn, then backed off to allow the other parishioners to get their refreshments after the late service. Standing along the wall where all the congregation's photos hung, she watched Samuel greet each person as they came into the rec hall. Her throat parched, she drank half the juice in several swallows. Over the past few days she had thought about the man more than she should. He and Jane had even plagued her dreams last night.

Jesse Blackburn approached with a cup of coffee. "So what do you think of our new minister?"

"Interesting sermon on redemption."

"He's a widower."

"Yes, I know and, Jesse, don't you get any ideas. As they say in the movies, I'm blowing this town come summer."

Taking a sip of her coffee, Jesse stared at her over the rim of her cup. "You are?"

"Don't act innocent. You know I've been planning this ever since Daniel decided to go to college."

Jesse leaned back against the wall, a picture in nonchalance. "It seems I recall you saying something about a vacation."

"It's more than a vacation. In fact, you'll have to do the annual Fourth of July auction this year, because I won't be here."

Her good friend splayed her hand across her chest. "You're leaving *me* in charge?"

"Don't sound so surprised. You and Darcy will do a great job."

"It won't be the same without you. You've been doing it for the past ten or so years."

"And I have made very good notes for you

to follow." Beth finished her punch, then crushed the paper cup into a ball. Frustration churned in her, making her feel as though she should shed her skin. "I'll help you until May. Then you're on your own."

"Boswell's a great organizer. I'll put him on it." Jesse straightened away from the wall. "Give the poor man something to do."

"How's it feel to have your own butler?"

Jesse laughed. "A bit funny, but Boswell's more like a member of the family than anything. Now, if I could just get him and Gramps to get along. Thank goodness Gramps married Susan Reed and lives at her place." She drained her coffee. "Are you sure you don't want me to have a little dinner party for the new reverend?"

"I think you *should* have a party."

Jesse's eyes widened. "You do?"

"To help introduce him to the whole congregation, not just the single women." Beth scanned the room for the man under discussion. He stood a few feet from the door, dressed in a black suit that accorded a nice contrast to his blond hair. The intent expression on his face while listening to Tanya Bolton gave Beth the impression he was a good listener, which was probably beneficial considering the needs of the people in the church. "What makes you think he's looking for a woman?"

"The romantic in me. I just hate seeing people alone."

"Jesse, I'm not alone. I have three siblings—who I grant you don't live with me anymore, but are still around. And I have my friends. Reverend Morgan has three children. And I met his aunt this morning in Sunday-school class. She lives with him. That certainly isn't alone."

"Boy, you need a man worse than I thought if you think children and an aunt are the same thing as a spouse."

"What are you two conspiring about?" Darcy Markham paused next to Beth, her hand at the small of her back.

Relieved at her friend's timely interruption, Beth smiled. "When are you going to have that baby?"

"I wish any minute, but the doctor says another month. Maybe I'll have it on my anniversary. If this child is anything like my son, he will take his sweet time. I'm not sure who is more anxious, me or Joshua."

"I sympathize with you two, but I'm glad it's you and not me." Beth's gaze caught Reverend Morgan moving away from the door and making his rounds to the various groups in the room.

"Well, I should hope so. You aren't married," Jesse said with a laugh.

Heat singed Beth's cheeks. "You know what I mean. I'm too old to have children. Besides, after raising my two brothers and sister, I'm through." After she'd turned thirty-five with no prospect of a husband, she'd given up hope of having her own children.

"Too old!" Darcy shifted her stance, rubbing her back. "You're only thirty-eight. Beth, if that's too old, then Jesse and I don't have long before we're over the hill."

"She's gonna be too busy traveling. She's leaving Sweetwater this summer and has informed me that we'll have to be in charge of the annual auction."

"Us?" Darcy pointed to her chest, then rested her hand on her stomach.

"Yes, you two. In fact, you and your husbands are invited to a party I'm having next weekend."

"A party? Isn't that Jesse's domain? You don't give parties."

Beth narrowed her eyes on Darcy, pressing her lips together. She had always been so predictable. That was about to change. "I am now. It's a celebration. I'm going to choose where I'm going this summer."

"Choose?" Jesse's brow furrowed.

"You two will just have to wait and see how. Can I count on you all coming to the celebration?"

Both Darcy and Jesse nodded their heads, big grins on their faces.

"Celebration?"

At the sound of the deep, gruff voice behind her, Beth blinked, then swallowed to coat her suddenly dry throat while the reverend stepped into view.

"I just wanted to thank you again, Beth, for rescuing Jane and me the other day." Samuel Morgan extended his hand toward her.

She fitted hers within his and shook it, aware of the curiosity of her two friends. "It was nothing."

Still holding her hand, Samuel smiled, the warmth in his expression reaching deep into his chocolate-colored eyes. "So what are you celebrating?"

Chapter Two

My great escape, Beth thought, but decided not to voice that answer. "This is the celebration I told you about. I'm planning a long vacation and having a party to celebrate the fact."

"That's as good a reason as any to have a celebration." Samuel finally released his hold on her hand.

"You're invited if you want to come. It's next Saturday night at my house." When Beth thought she saw hesitation in his eyes, she hastened to add, "It'll be a good way for you to get to know some of the congregation in a less formal environment." Now, why had she said that? That had always been Jesse's role.

"Darcy and I will be there along with our husbands." Jesse shot a look toward Darcy that conveyed a message that Beth couldn't see. "I'll volunteer to help you with the preparations, Beth, since giving dinner parties is my specialty."

Beth knew she would have to put a stop to her friend's matchmaking scheme that she could almost see percolating in her mind. She couldn't very well exclude the reverend after he'd overheard their discussion of her celebration. Yeah, right.

"I can help, too," Darcy said, rubbing her stomach. "We can meet at your house for our Saturday-morning get-together instead of at Alice's Café."

Beth forced a smile to her lips. "Thanks," she murmured, again noticing a nonverbal exchange between Darcy and Jesse.

"Oh, I see Nick waving to me. Got to go." Jesse hugged Beth and Darcy goodbye and hurried away.

"And I need to sit down. I'm going to find Joshua and a quiet corner to rest in." Darcy kissed Beth on the cheek, then nodded toward Samuel before lumbering toward her husband, who was leaning against the piano.

That was the fastest getaway her two friends had ever made. Beth made a mental note to call them and set them straight the second she got home from church. She was not looking for a man. Didn't they know she was the plain town spinster who was a good twenty or thirty pounds overweight?

"Since that just leaves you and me, can we talk a moment in private?"

You and me. Those simple words conjured up all kinds of visions that mocked her earlier words that she wasn't looking to date. "Sure. Is something wrong?"

Samuel gestured toward an area away from the crowd in the rec hall, an alcove with a padded bench that offered them a more quiet environment. He sat, and waited for her to do the same. She stared at the small space that allowed only two people to sit comfortably—and the reverend was a large man who took up more than his half of the bench. While she debated whether to stand or sit, a perplexed expression descended on his face. If it hadn't been for Jesse insisting on fixing her up with Samuel, she wouldn't be undecided about something as simple as sitting and talking with him, she thought.

With a sigh she sat, her leg and arm brushing against his. Awareness—a sensation she didn't deal with often—bolted through her. "What do you need to discuss?"

"Jane. She won't let me help her with her

homework." He rubbed the palms of his hands together. "I'm at a loss as to what to do with her. Any suggestions?"

"Let me see how we do tomorrow when she stays after school. At the beginning of every year I give a learning-styles inventory to see how each student learns. I haven't had a chance to give it to Jane yet, but I will this week. I'll know more after that."

"Learning styles?"

"Whether she's a visual, auditory or kinesthetic learner. Then I can use that information to teach her the way she learns best."

"I appreciate any help you can give me. I suspect tomorrow when I talk with her other teachers I'm going to find she hasn't done any work for them, either."

"You said she hasn't taken her mother's death well. Have you considered counseling?"

"Tried that, and she wouldn't talk to a stranger. She just sat there, most of the time not saying a word."

"How about someone she knows?"

"Aunt Mae has tried and Jane just clammed up." He rubbed his thumb into his palm. "I've tried and haven't done much better. Jane has always been an introvert. She doesn't express her emotions much."

"Let me see what I can do," Beth said, knowing she didn't have long before she would be gone. Four months might not be long enough to establish a relationship with the teenager and get her to open up about what was bothering her. She would encourage Jane to go to the school counselor. Zoey Witherspoon was very good at her job.

Samuel rose. "I appreciate any help," he repeated. "I'm a desperate dad."

"I hear that frequently. I teach fifteen-year-olds who have raging hormones. They fluctuate between being a child and an adult, from being dependent on their parents to being independent of them."

"I was a teenager once, not that long ago, but frankly it didn't prepare me for dealing with my daughter. I think I might have a better handle on Craig when he becomes a teenager." He chuckled. "At least I hope so, since that's only a year away."

"I know what you mean. I raised two brothers and a sister. My sister was easier for me. I struggled with Daniel, my youngest brother. I'm surprised he made it through high school. He failed several subjects and had to go to school a semester longer than his classmates. I will say I saw him grow up a lot in the past six months. I think watching all his friends go off to college last summer while he had to return to high school sobered him and made him aware of some of the mistakes he'd made."

Samuel placed a hand on her arm. "Thank you."

The touch of his fingers seared her. She knew she was overreacting to the gesture, but she couldn't stop her heart from pounding against her chest. She was afraid its loud thumping could be heard across the rec hall. Even before she'd begun raising her siblings she hadn't dated much. She was plain and shy, not two aspects that drew scores of men.

"You're welcome," she finally answered, her lips, mouth and throat dry. And she had been the one to invite him to her party next Saturday night.

Jane slammed the book closed. "How are you supposed to look a word up in the dictionary when you don't have any idea how to spell it?" She slouched back in her desk, defiance in her expression.

Beth glanced up from grading a paper. "What word?"

"Perspective."

"How do you think you spell it?"

"I don't know!" The girl's frustration etched a deep frown into her features.

Beth rose and came around her desk to stand next to Jane's. "What do you think it starts with?"

"I don't—" Jane's eyes narrowed, and she looked toward the window. "With a *p*." Her gaze returned to Beth's. "But there are *thousands* of words that start with *p*."

"Let's start with the first syllable. Per."

"*P-r*—" Jane pinched her lips together, her brows slashing downward.

"Almost. It's *p-e-r*. What do you think comes next? Per*spec*tive."

Jane leaned forward, folding her arms over the dictionary. "At this rate I'll get one paragraph written by this time tomorrow. What's the use?"

"I have a dictionary of commonly misspelled words. I can lend it to you. It might help with some of the words. If it does, you can get your own copy. See if you can find it by looking up *p-e-r-s-p*." Beth knew it would be a lot faster and easier on everyone if she spelled the word completely for Jane, but she wanted to see how the teenager did. She had a feeling a lot more was going on with the young woman. Not only did she have few word attack skills, but she read with difficulty.

Jane blew out a breath and flipped the dictionary open, thumbing through the pages until she found the *p* section. With only a handful of selections to choose from, Jane pointed and said, "There." She pushed the dictionary to the side and wrote down the word, grumbling about the time it had taken to find it.

Beth made her way back to her desk. Jane had been struggling with the writing assignment for an hour. The past few days working with her after school had sent red flags waving concerning Jane's academic ability. Beth decided that when Samuel came to pick up his daughter she would have a talk with him about Jane.

Not ten minutes later Beth knew the instant Samuel appeared in the doorway. As though she had a sixth sense when it came to the man, she looked up to find him smiling at her from across the room. A dimple appeared in his left cheek, drawing Beth's attention.

The second Jane saw him she finished the sentence she had been writing and gathered up her papers. She started to slide from the desk.

"Are you through, Jane?" Samuel asked, entering.

His presence seemed to shrink the large classroom to the size of a small closet, and for the life of her, Beth couldn't understand why her pulse began to race. She suddenly worried that she looked as if she had spent the whole day in front of 150 students trying to inspire them to love literature—which she had. She felt even plainer, and wheeled her chair closer to her desk to shield her rather drab dress of gray cotton that didn't quite hide her extra pounds. Maybe she should buy a few new outfits, more updated with some splashes of color, she thought.

"Yes." Jane rose and brought the paper to Beth's desk. After plopping it down, she headed for the door. "I'm getting a drink of water and going to my locker."

The tension that churned the air left with Jane. Samuel watched his daughter disappear through the doorway before he turned toward Beth with one brow arched.

"This writing assignment was very difficult for her." Beth picked up Jane's paper and skimmed it. "And from the looks of it, she doesn't have a firm background in grammar, punctuation and spelling. Her thoughts on the subject are good ones, but she has a hard time getting them down on paper."

Samuel covered the distance between them and hovered in front of Beth's desk— way too close for her peace of mind. The dimple in his left cheek vanished as he frowned.

"What are you telling me?" He took Jane's paper and began to read.

"I think Jane needs to be tested to see if she has a learning disability."

His head shot up, his gaze riveted to hers. "A learning disability!"

"A learning disability doesn't mean that Jane isn't smart. People with normal, even high, IQs can have a learning disability that hinders them learning what they need to know. How's she doing in her other classes?"

"Not well except for geometry. She's got an A in that class. That and advanced drawing."

"Is she doing the work for the other teachers?"

"No. The same as yours. I'm trying to help her every night. She can't do anything until she gets her homework done, which basically takes her the whole evening. The Morgan household has not been a fun one this past week. I feel more like a drill sergeant than a father."

Disregarding how she imagined she looked, Beth stood, feeling at a disadvantage sitting behind her desk. She came around beside Samuel, wanting to help, to comfort. "I think she struggles with the reading part. When I gave her the learning-styles inventory, she tested almost completely a visual learner. So much of the work in high school is from lectures. I'm not sure she's getting it. Her auditory skills seem to be weak."

"Then what do I need to do?"

"Sign permission for her to be tested. I'll refer her and our school psychologist will contact you."

"I don't know how well Jane will take this."

Beth touched his arm, the urge to comfort growing stronger the longer she was around this man. There was something about him that conveyed a troubled soul, and she had never been able to turn away from someone in need. "This can all be handled without the other students knowing."

"I don't have a choice."

As his gaze locked with hers, Beth forgot where she was for a moment. Finally when she shook off the effect he had on her senses, she said, "You always have a choice. But if she's having trouble reading it's better to know now than later."

"You don't think it's normal teenage rebellion?"

"No. I think she's using her defiant attitude as a way to cover up not knowing."

"Then refer her."

"Do you want me to talk to Jane about what I'm doing?"

"No, that's my job. I'll talk with her on the way home. I don't want her to be surprised."

"I'll be glad to help any way I can."

Again his gaze snared hers, drawing her in. "You've already done so much."

"Dad, aren't you coming?" Framed in the doorway, Jane slung her backpack over her left shoulder.

"Yes. I'll be by this time tomorrow to pick her up."

Samuel left the classroom, with his daughter walking ahead of him at a fast clip. When he stepped outside, the brisk winter air blasted him in the face. Snow still blanketed the ground, but the roads had been cleared. He found his daughter in the passenger seat of his Ford Mustang, her eyes closed, her head resting against the cushion. For a few seconds he took in her calm expression, which of late was rare, and regretted the conversation to come. But Jane needed to know what was going to happen.

Samuel started the car and drove out of the school parking lot. *Lord, I know I haven't visited with You as I should. But I need help with Jane. Please help me to find the right words to explain about the testing. Please help me to understand what is happening with my daughter.*

"What were you and Miss Coleman talking about?" Jane sat up, watching the landscape out the side window.

He took a deep, composing breath. "She wants to refer you for testing and I told her to go ahead."

Jane twisted toward him. "Testing? What kind?"

"She thinks you're struggling to read and that you might have a learning disability."

"I'm not dumb!"

"She didn't say that and I'm not, either. Your A in geometry proves that. But something's going on, Jane. Don't you want to find out what it is?"

"I'm not dumb!" Tears glistened in his daughter's eyes.

Shaken by the sight of her tears, Samuel parked his car in his driveway. Jane rarely cried. He started to reach for her to comfort her, but she glared at him. Swiping the back of her hand across her cheeks, she shoved the door open, bolted from the car and ran toward the house.

He gripped the steering wheel and let his head sag until it touched the cold plastic. He hadn't handled that well. Like everything else the past few years, he was fumbling to find the correct path. He felt as though he were lost in the desert, wandering around trying to find the promised land.

"I'm so glad you could come a little early." Beth held open the door and stepped to the side to allow Jesse into her house.

"Am I imagining things or was that panic in your voice a little while ago?" Jesse asked, following her through the living room into the dining room.

"You know I don't entertain much. I don't even know why I decided to have this party. I've got the house clean. That was easy. But do I have enough food for everyone?" Beth gestured toward the table that could seat eight if the leaf was in it, which it was.

Jesse's eyes grew round. "What color is the tablecloth? I can't tell. You've got so much food on it."

"Are you trying to tell me I overdid it?"

"How many people did you invite? The whole congregation plus the staff you work with?"

"I don't want anyone going hungry."

"Believe me, if they do, they have an eating disorder."

Beth scanned the table laden with three cakes, two pies, several dozen cookies and brownies, vegetable and fruit trays with two different dips each, several kinds of small sandwiches without the crust, crackers and chips with assorted spreads and a cheese ball. "I had to put the drinks in the kitchen. I ran out of room."

Jesse snatched up a carrot stick and took a bite. "So how many people are coming?"

"Besides you and Nick, Darcy and Joshua, there are the reverend, Tanya Bolton, Zoey Witherspoon, Paul Howard and Boswell."

"Boswell? He didn't say anything to me about coming."

"I saw him at the grocery yesterday when I was buying some of the food and thought he might enjoy coming. You don't mind, do you?"

"No, especially since Nate and Cindy are over at Gramps and Susan's. I'm glad Boswell's getting out. I've felt guilty about uprooting him from Chicago. He promises me that he doesn't mind living in Sweetwater, but I'm not sure I believe him." Jesse popped a potato chip into her mouth. "What do you want me to help you with?"

Beth twirled. "Do I look all right?"

"Why, Beth Coleman, I've never known you to care too much about how you look."

Regretting that she had given in to her panic and called Jesse for advice, Beth started toward the kitchen. She realized she was plain, but that didn't mean she didn't care about how she appeared to others. *Come on, Beth, don't you really mean Samuel Morgan?*

"You can wipe that smug smile off your face, Jesse. I just didn't want to be overdressed."

Jesse stopped Beth's progress with a hand on her shoulder. "I'll be serious. Turn around."

Beth faced her friend, her hands on her waist, now hoping she could pull off an "I don't care" attitude.

With a finger against her chin, Jesse studied her. "Black jeans with a cream silk blouse. Not bad. New blouse?"

The heat of a blush scored Beth's cheeks. "Yes. I haven't bought anything new in months." And except for an occasional treat to herself for Christmas and her birthday, she purchased only the basic necessities she needed for school. While her siblings had been growing up, clothing had been expensive, not to mention later helping with their college tuition.

Holding up her hands, Jesse took a step back. "Stop right there. I'm glad you're finally doing something for yourself and not just for your brothers and sister. It's about time." Her gaze skimmed the length of Beth once more. "Deep-six the tennis shoes. Heels would be better with what you have on."

"Tennis shoes go with jeans."

"But heels will look better with your blouse, which is soft and feminine. Don't you have a black pair we got last year?"

"They're awfully dressy. This is a casual party."

Jesse flipped her hand in the air, dismissing Beth's concerns. "You'll be casually elegant."

The sound of the doorbell cut through the sudden silence.

Beads of perspiration popped out on Beth's upper lip. She didn't give parties. Why had she come up with this way to kick off her new outlook on life? Bad, bad idea.

Jesse waved her toward her bedroom. "Go. I'll get the door. I don't want to see those tennis shoes."

Wiping her hand across her upper lip, Beth hurried away, wondering if she could hide for at least an hour in her bedroom. She would have been fine with just Darcy, Joshua, Jesse and Nick. She could have convinced herself that this wasn't a party she was responsible for, but the additional five people made a mockery out of that thought.

While rifling through the bottom of her closet for the box that held her black heels, she heard laughter coming from her living room and the doorbell chiming again. When she finally found the shoes, stuck way in the back, she examined them, unable to believe she had bought them. It was Jesse's fault. She'd worn them only once—to Darcy's wedding. Jesse had been with her when she had purchased them. In fact, Jesse had been the one who had insisted she buy them. On her own she never would have, and still couldn't believe she'd let Jesse talk her into them. Beth held them up, still debating whether to wear the silk-and-leather heels.

They were three inches high—two more than she usually wore—with long pointed toes and no back strap. They looked uncomfortable, but actually—much to her surprise when she had tried them on at the store—they were very comfortable.

When the bell announced another arrival, Beth kicked off her tennis shoes and removed her socks, then donned the black heels. She didn't dare look at herself in her full-length mirror. She *knew* she wouldn't leave the room if she did. Hurrying as quickly as possible in her heels, she came into the foyer as Jesse opened the door to another guest—Reverend Samuel Morgan.

He peered past Jesse toward Beth and for the barest moment his eyes flashed surprise. The hammering of her heart increased, worry nibbling at her composure. What did she look like? She'd tried some new makeup she'd gotten at the grocery store yesterday and had left her curly hair down about her shoulders, probably in a wild mess by now. She wanted to whirl around, go back to her bedroom and check her appearance in her full-length mirror.

Then he smiled and her world tilted for a few seconds.

After murmuring a greeting to Jesse, Samuel came toward Beth, his long strides purposeful as if he were a man on a mission. "Thank you for including me in your celebration." He clasped her hand between his and shook it. "I haven't had a chance to do much since moving here. As you suggested, it'll be nice to meet some of my congregation in a relaxed atmosphere."

Relaxed atmosphere? There was nothing remotely relaxed about her at the moment. "I'm glad you could come." Her hand was still sandwiched between his. Suddenly she didn't feel thirty-eight but a young woman of eighteen, inexperienced but eager to learn the ways of dating. That was not to say she hadn't dated a few men over the years, but most of her time had been taken up with caring for her siblings and trying to make ends meet, first as a college student and then on the meager pay of a teacher. She definitely felt like a novice.

Finally releasing her hand, Samuel peeked into the living room, which also gave him a view of the dining-room table loaded with food. "Is everyone here?"

Beth scanned the small group of friends and nodded. "I like to cook and I just kept preparing food until I ran out of time." She actually had missed not cooking for others since Daniel had left for college.

"I'm glad I didn't have time to eat dinner before coming."

"So am I. I don't know what I'm going to do with this after you all leave."

"Freeze it," Jesse said, approaching them.

"I don't have a big enough freezer. You all are going to have to take some home with you."

"Did I hear correctly? We'll be taking doggie bags home with us?" Joshua asked, helping Darcy onto the couch.

Darcy laughed, shifting to get as comfortable as possible for a woman eight months pregnant. "I still haven't mastered the art of cooking, and poor Liz and Dad get tired of us coming to eat with them at the farm."

Joshua sat next to his wife and took her hand. "She's become quite good with one or two dishes. Sean and I don't order pizza nearly like we used to."

Darcy playfully punched Joshua on the arm. "I'm not that bad. I can prepare more than one or two."

Beth leaned close to Samuel, and immediately realized her mistake when she got a whiff of his citrusy aftershave. "Yes, she is. Just remember that when planning anything having to do with food at the church."

"I heard that, Beth Coleman. I thought you were my friend."

The laughter in Darcy's voice took the sting out of her words. "I'll give you two doggie bags, Joshua."

"Thanks. You're a good woman, Beth."

She was used to the ribbing among her and her friends, but with Samuel next to her, she couldn't help feeling as though she were on stage in front of a whole group of strangers. And that was something she avoided at all costs. She was a behind-the-scenes kind of person, never wanting to be in the limelight like Jesse and even Darcy.

"Please, everyone get a plate and eat. The drinks are in the kitchen," Beth announced, aware of Samuel's every move next to her. She felt his gaze on her and wanted to escape. She knew both Jesse and Darcy would never allow her to. This was why she didn't give parties, she remembered—too late.

"I believe you know everyone here, Samuel." Beth gestured toward her guests. "I need to see if there's enough ice for the drinks." She practically ran from the man, making a beeline for the kitchen and, she hoped, time to regroup. If she had thought this party thing through, she would have invited at least half a dozen more people, she thought. She was afraid Jesse would begin to pair everyone off and find there was no one for Samuel except either Tanya or her.

In the kitchen Boswell placed ice into his glass from the bucket that Beth had already filled. He glanced toward her when she entered.

"Do you have everything you need?" she asked, relieved he was the only one in the room.

Jesse and Nick's British manservant poured diet soda into his glass. "I swore I would never drink this stuff, but alas, the pounds are beginning to show. I can't believe I've been forced to this."

Beth suppressed a smile. "There's always water."

"You have bottled water?"

"Well, no. But the water from the tap is fine."

Horror flitted across his face. "I'll drink this."

As he left, Beth said, "And don't forget to

eat. I'm sure there's something on the table that isn't fattening."

The second he was gone, Beth released a long sigh, relishing the quiet of the kitchen. Then the door swung open and Tanya entered. "I almost ran into Boswell. If it wasn't for his quick reflexes, he would have dropped his drink."

"I'd better prop the door open or there'll be an accident."

While Tanya sailed past her to the counter where the drinks were, Beth retrieved a brick she used when she wanted to leave the swinging door open between the kitchen and the dining room. As she straightened from placing it at the base of the door, she took a step back and collided with a solid wall of flesh. The scent of citrus drifted to her, and she knew Samuel was behind her.

She fixed a smile on her face and turned. "Can I get you anything to drink? I've got sodas, iced tea, decaf coffee and fruit punch. And of course, there's water." Nerves stretched taut, she listened to herself speak so fast she wondered if Samuel even understood what she said. He looked a little dazed. "Oh, and I forgot. I have hot apple cider on the stove," she added a lot more slowly.

"That sounds nice. But I can get it."

Tanya breezed by. "Beth, I'm filling in for Darcy in her Sunday-school class until after the baby comes."

"Great," Beth said to Tanya's back as she disappeared into the dining room.

"She has so much energy." Samuel followed Beth to the stove and watched her ladle a steaming cup of apple cider into a blue ceramic mug.

"That's Tanya." She poured some cider for herself.

Samuel leaned back against the counter and took a tentative sip of his drink, surveying the kitchen. "I like your home. Very cozy."

"And small. Not now, but when my brothers and sister lived here, we met ourselves coming and going. One bathroom and four people isn't what I call an ideal situation." She was chattering again—most uncharacteristic.

"You raised all your siblings?" Samuel appeared relaxed and comfortable as though he was going to stay a while. He crossed his legs at the ankles and grasped the edge of the counter with one hand.

Dressed in black slacks and a striped gray-and-maroon shirt, he filled her kitchen with his large presence, someone who quietly commanded people's attention. She still marveled that he was a minister, when he looked more like a linebacker or a well-trained soldier. Did he work out? That question surprised her and made her gasp.

Samuel cocked his head, his brow furrowed. "Something wrong?"

She shook her head, berating herself for the folly of her thoughts. "Forgot something." *My brain,* she thought, realizing she hadn't really lied to her preacher.

"Can I help?"

"No, everything's under control." *Just as soon as I stop thinking about you.* "To answer your question, yes, I raised my brothers and sister. I was nineteen when my mother died in childbirth, and I wasn't going to let the state take them away from our home, such as it is."

"Where was your father?"

She should have realized he would ask that question. She bit the inside of her mouth, trying to transfer the mental pain she felt when her father was mentioned to a physical one instead. It didn't work. Even after nineteen years her father's abandonment bored into her heart, leaving a gaping hole she wasn't sure would ever totally heal. "He left us when my mother was six months pregnant with their fourth child. He walked out one day and we never heard from him again."

Samuel straightened from the counter. "I'm sorry. I know how inadequate those words can be at times, but it's never easy when a parent abandons a child."

"That's why I would never abandon my brothers and sister to let some stranger raise them."

"That was quite a task to take on by yourself at nineteen. You didn't have any relatives to help you?"

"We're a small family. My father had an uncle who tried to help some when he could, but he was old and sct in his ways. Both of my parents were only children. My mother used to say that's why she wanted a houseful of kids. I guess my father didn't feel that way." The intense pressure in her chest made each breath difficult. She drew in several deep gulps of air, but nothing seemed to relieve the constriction. She hadn't thought about her father in a long time—most people knew it was a subject she didn't discuss.

"I can see I've distressed you." He took a step toward her, reaching to touch her arm in comfort.

She backed up against the refrigerator, feeling trapped by the kindness in his expression. "You would think I'd be over it after nineteen years."

His arm fell to his side. "No, I don't know if a child ever totally gets over a parent walking out on her. It's hard enough on a child when one parent dies. Even though the parent doesn't choose to die, the child still experiences abandonment."

"Not just the child but the spouse, too."

The air vibrated with suppressed tension, the focus of the conversation shifting.

For a few seconds a haunted look dimmed his dark eyes, then he managed to veil his expression by lowering his lashes. "Yes."

Chapter Three

"You know, in here—" Samuel tapped the side of his head "—I know that my wife didn't choose to leave us. But in here—" he splayed his hand over his heart "—it doesn't make any difference. Pain is pain."

Beth swallowed the tightness swelling in her throat. "I think Jane's feeling the same emotions."

"I know she is. She was very close to Ruth and took her death especially hard."

But not as hard as you, Beth thought, seeing his anguish reflected in the depths of his eyes.

"Then we moved not long after that happened, and that was when I decided to resign from the army. Moving around was becoming too hard on my family, especially without their mother."

"What made you become a chaplain in the army?"

"I wanted to serve my country and God. I thought I could do it by being an army chaplain."

"But now you don't think so?" She'd heard the doubt in his voice and wondered about it.

"I discovered you can't serve two masters—at least, not me." He turned away and walked to the stove to refill his mug.

The sight of his back, his shoulders stiff with tension, told Beth that topic of conversation was finished. She could respect that. There were a lot of things she wouldn't discuss with others, and she and Samuel were practically strangers.

Even though the last thing she felt like doing at the moment was smiling, she did, needing to lighten the mood. "Tanya reminded me of something we'll need to talk about soon."

He threw her a glance over his shoulder, then slowly pivoted. "What?"

"I run the Sunday School, and since I'll be leaving in the summer, we should discuss a replacement so I can train that person this spring." She found if she voiced her plans out loud the reality of leaving Sweetwater became more real.

"Nothing like the present."

"Here? Now?"

"Well, not exactly right this minute, but how about next week some time? Why don't you come to Friday-night dinner at my house? Aunt Mae goes all out that night. For some reason she thinks we should celebrate the end of a work week. I don't think she understands I do a lot of my work on the weekend. But it's something she's done for years and I didn't have the heart to change it when she came to live with us."

"I hate to intrude on a family evening."

"Nonsense. If I entertain, it's usually then." Samuel sipped his cider, his gaze intent upon her.

The refrigerator still propped her up. Beth pushed away, surprised by the trembling in her legs—as though their conversation had affected her more than she cared to admit. "What time?"

"Six-thirty."

"Fine." She hoped she could stay awake long enough to hold an intelligent conversation. Friday nights were usually her crash night after a long week of teaching. She often would wake up around eleven, having fallen asleep in front of the television and having no idea what had been on the set earlier in the evening. "Speaking of celebrations, I think it's time I threw my dart."

"You really are going to decide where you go by throwing a dart?"

The incredulous tone of his voice made her laugh. "Yup."

Beth walked through the dining room, encouraging everyone to have a seat in the living room. Her nine guests crowded into the small area, with Jesse sitting on the arm of the lounge chair that Nick occupied and Tanya on the floor next to the sofa.

Beth went into the foyer and retrieved from the closet a tagboard and one dart. "As you can see, this is a map of Central and South America. I'm planning a trip and tonight I'm deciding where. I'd ask someone to hold the board up, but I'm afraid I might be a bit wild with the dart, so instead I'll position it on the rocking chair if Zoey doesn't mind standing for a moment—unless you want to hold it."

Her friend from school stopped rocking and leaped from the chair, horror on her face. "I'll pass. I've seen you play sports." To the group she added, "I would suggest everyone give her plenty of room. No telling where the dart will end up. I can remember the church softball game where she hit me and I wasn't anywhere near where she intended to throw the ball."

"Oh, yeah. You had a bruise on your leg for weeks after that," Darcy said, scooting closer to Joshua on the couch so Zoey could sit next to her.

Beth positioned herself in front of the tag-board, then turned around to her guests. "Hence the warning."

Several nearest her backed away. Beth squared off in front of the rocking chair, squeezed her eyes closed and tossed the dart. It clanged to the tile floor in the foyer.

"If you miss the map, does that mean you stay, Beth?" asked Paul Howard, an assistant principal at her school.

She started toward the dart. Samuel picked it up first and handed it to her. Their gazes touched for a long moment, humor deep in his eyes. She liked the way they crinkled at the corners. She liked their color—it reminded her of a piece of dark, rich chocolate that she loved to eat.

"No," she murmured, suddenly aware of the silence in the room. "It only means I try again."

Boswell and Paul moved back even farther. Half the room was clear for her next shot. Beth shook her head, closed her eyes and threw the dart without really giving it much thought, still rattled by the silent exchange a moment before with Samuel. It plunked into the tagboard. She eased one eye open and saw the dart in the middle of the map.

"Brazil." Zoey came to stand beside her and stare at the map. "Guess you'd better get some Portuguese tapes instead of the Spanish ones."

"The Amazon. How do you like heat and humidity?" Paul asked, stepping next to Zoey.

"Not to mention snakes and other unpleasant animals. Are you going to throw again?" Jesse flanked her on the other side.

With so much of South America being taken up by the Amazon, why am I surprised the dart landed there? Beth wondered. "No, I'm not going to throw again. Brazil it will be."

A mild "heat" wave had tempered the bitter cold of the past few weeks, pushing the temperature up to near fifty. But with dusk approaching quickly, the air began to chill and the sun was low behind the trees. Beth paused on her porch and looked across her brown lawn, the drabness fitting her mood perfectly. Her feet ached from standing more than usual that week at school and her mind felt muddled from the late nights she'd spent grading writing assignments until her eyes had crossed and the words had blurred.

All she wanted to do was collapse into her soft velour lounge chair, switch on her television for background noise and stare unseeing at the screen. Do nothing. For once. But this was Friday and she had told Samuel she would come to dinner. With a heavy sigh, she stuck her key into the lock and opened her front door.

A noise from the back of the house alerted her that someone was inside. She tensed, her hand clenched around the knob.

"Beth, is that you?"

Relief sagged her body against the door. Daniel was home from college. "Yes."

Her youngest brother came down the hall, drying his hair with a blue towel, wearing a pair of jeans slung low. "I just took a shower and was getting dressed to go out."

She managed to close the front door without slamming it, a remarkable feat of patience when she didn't think she had any left. "I didn't know you were coming home this weekend."

"I caught a ride with Mitch. He's taking me back on Sunday, too, so you don't need to."

"Oh." Her exhausted mind couldn't come up with anything else to say while she stared at her brother.

He hung the towel over his shoulder. "In fact, he'll be by in fifteen minutes. We're going to Pete's."

She refrained from saying "oh" again by mashing her lips together.

"We'll talk tomorrow. I'll tell you about my classes then." He turned and headed down the hall toward his bedroom.

Beth watched him disappear, irritated at herself because she was irritated at Daniel for not telling her he was coming home for the weekend. She should be happy—and she was—but he had a way of taking over the whole house. To emphasize her thought, loud music blared from his room, chasing away the silence she desired after a day spent listening to 150 students.

When she placed her stuffed briefcase and

purse on the table in the foyer, she noticed the mail that Daniel must have brought into the house. On top was an envelope from the Christian Mission Institute. She tore into it with a jolt of energy. A letter welcoming her interest in their overseas program and an application caused her hands to tremble. When she filled this out, she'd be one step closer.

As she stared at the application, an image of Samuel came into her mind—of a look of vulnerability that she had seen beneath his confident surface. A man in need of a friend. Surprised by that thought, she put the letter and application on the table next to her purse. She would deal with it later when she wasn't so tired, when she wasn't picturing a man who shouldn't send her heart pounding with a smile.

Beth walked to the kitchen to find a drink with some caffeine in it. She rummaged around in the refrigerator, positive that she'd had one cola left. Nothing. She scanned the counter and discovered the empty can by the sink along with a dirty plate and fork. Daniel.

For a brief moment she thought of making a pot of coffee and drinking it all, but decided instead to take a cool shower. Maybe that would help keep her awake while having dinner at Samuel's. Then she again visualized the handsome reverend and knew she wouldn't have any trouble staying awake, because for the past few weeks he'd haunted her dreams when she'd finally fallen asleep.

Why now? She'd never been particularly interested in a man to the point she dreamed about him.

She wasn't getting enough rest. That had to be it. Shaking her head as if that would rid her mind of the man, she started for her bedroom. Passing the laundry room, she caught sight of a *huge* mound of clothes thrown on its floor and covering most of it. Daniel. Now she knew her brother's real reason for coming home. He hadn't done any laundry since she'd dropped him off three weeks ago. Flipping on the light, she picked up a dark shirt that reeked of smoke and cologne and waded through the pile of clothes to the washer. She dropped it in, followed by another and another.

Finished with his sermon for the coming Sunday, Samuel pushed back his chair at his desk in his office and began to rise when a knock sounded at his door. "Yes?"

Tanya Bolton strode into the room. "Do you have a few minutes to talk to me?"

The troubled expression in her eyes prompted Samuel to say, "Yes, of course. What's wrong?" He gestured toward a chair.

Her eyes took on a misty look as she fought tears. She sank into the chair next to his desk. "Tom has been hurt."

"Tom?"

"My husband." Tanya folded her hands in her lap and stared at them. "He's in prison for arson. A while back he was caught burning barns in the area." She lifted her gaze to his. "He's a good man, really. He just went a little crazy after our daughter's accident. As you know, Crystal is in a wheelchair. She fell from a horse and became paralyzed. He blamed all horses after that."

"How was he hurt?" Samuel asked, realizing there was so much he didn't know about his congregation and that this put him at a disadvantage when dealing with his parishioners' problems.

"An inmate attacked him and stabbed him. He's in the infirmary. The doctor says he'll be okay, but, Reverend Morgan, I'm worried. Lately Tom has said he doesn't want me to come visit him anymore. He's never let our daughter come. I don't know what to do." Tanya twisted her hands together, the sheen of tears visible in her eyes. "I'm so afraid for Tom, my daughter, myself. What should I do?"

The question he most feared was spoken. There had been a time when Samuel had always had a ready answer, had been sure of the advice he'd given. Now he felt as though he was fumbling around in the dark, most often stumbling and falling.

"He needs me now more than ever and he won't see me." A tear slipped from Tanya's eye.

Lord, help me to say and do the right thing, Samuel prayed, aware of the silence that shouldn't have filled the office. Tanya stared at him, waiting for an answer to her problem.

"Sometimes we have to honor a person's wishes even when we don't think they are good for them. Have you prayed for guidance?"

Tanya nodded. "That's why I'm here."

Panic took hold of Samuel. Counseling was a natural part of his job, but since his wife's death he'd felt inadequate, now more than ever. How could he counsel another when he couldn't help himself?

Samuel offered his hands to Tanya. "Let's pray together."

Tanya took his hands and bowed her head. Samuel began to pray, hoping the words would soothe a troubled soul.

Beth fingered the tortoiseshell clip that held her riotous damp hair pulled back. A few strands of her unruly mop had come loose and curled about her face. Long ago she'd given up trying to control it, and spending hours straightening it seemed like a waste of time, time she'd never had for herself. Peering down at her black jeans and heavy black-and-white sweater, she satisfied herself she was ready to ring the bell. She'd done all she could to make herself presentable in her rush to be on time for dinner, but there wasn't much she could do with her plain features. She'd started to press the buzzer when the door swept open and warmth enveloped her.

The bright lights of his foyer framed Samuel, throwing his face into the shadows, but Beth saw the smile of greeting. The welcome in his expression rivaled the warmth emanating from his house, drawing her in out of the cold.

"I hope I'm not too late. My brother unexpectedly arrived home from college with tons of laundry to be done this weekend. I wanted to get a jump start on it."

"He doesn't do his own?" After she stepped across the threshold, Samuel closed the front door behind Beth.

"His one attempt turned half his white underwear and T-shirts pink and cost a small fortune to replace." She winced at the defensive tone in her voice and tried to temper it with a grin. "It just seemed easier to do it myself. Less hassle."

Samuel started to say something, clamped his mouth closed and began to turn toward the living room. In midturn he paused and glanced over his shoulder. "Wearing pink underwear a few times will teach him pretty fast to do the laundry the correct way."

Beth bit down on her lower lip.

"I don't usually give advice unless asked." Samuel rushed on, a frown crinkling his forehead. "But he's what, eighteen, nineteen, and mostly on his own now. He needs to learn. When you leave this summer, who will do it then?"

"You haven't said anything that Jesse, Darcy and Zoey haven't told me. I know I'm enabling. But Daniel and I had a rough few years and I decided a long time ago to pick the battles I wanted to fight with him. Laundry wasn't one of them. School was."

"Is that issue better now?"

She nodded. "He finally sees the value in a good education."

"Then move on. You're doing him a big favor teaching him how to live on his own. I wish I had known. After Ruth's death I had to learn fast if I wanted our children to have clean clothes and to eat decent meals, not to mention live in a clean environment." Without another word Samuel stepped to the side to let her go before him into his large living room.

Beth had been in this house many times when Reverend Collins lived here, so she knew the layout well. But when she entered the room, surprise took hold of her. Gone was the formal decor of the previous occupant, to be replaced with a large, comfortable sofa of navy-and-maroon plaid. There were two overstuffed maroon chairs flanking an oversize table with a tall brass lamp. The furniture was a dark cherry, richly polished and gleaming in the soft lighting. The roaring fire in the fireplace completed the impression of homey comfort and pulled her forward.

"I like what you've done. Obviously you've gotten a lot unpacked."

"Not me so much as Aunt Mae with minor help from us, especially Craig and Allie. Once she arrived the boxes disappeared totally in a week's time. She has a way of getting the kids to do stuff that would make a drill sergeant envious."

"I bet she was popular on base."

His chuckle spiced the air. "Yeah. A few sergeants came calling, especially when she was cooking certain dishes. I usually had a guest at least a couple of times a week."

"Did that bother you?"

"I'd do anything to make my aunt happy. She was a lifesaver for us after my wife died." He backed away toward the entrance. "Excuse me while I find the rest of my family and let them know you're here. Dinner shouldn't be long. I hope you're hungry. I think Aunt Mae went overboard."

"It smells wonderful," Beth said, taking a deep breath of air laced with the scents of spices, onions and meat.

"Pot roast with potatoes and carrots. I can vouch that it's delicious." Samuel left, climbing the stairs.

The crackling of the fire and the ticking of the clock on the mantel were the only noises Beth heard for a moment. Then from upstairs the children's voices drifted to her. Someone dropped something along the lines of a bowling ball from the way it sounded. Now, that's more like a house with three children in it, she thought.

She turned to the fire and stretched her hands out to warm them. Scanning the family photographs on the mantel, Beth paused at a portrait of Samuel, his children and a beautiful woman, petite, with medium brown hair and sparkling dark eyes, dressed in a soft creation of turquoise-blue. His wife. Jane looked a lot like her, while Craig and Allie looked like their father. Ruth's beauty complemented Samuel's handsome face. They had been a stunning couple.

Beth glanced down at the bulky sweater that added a few more pounds to a body already overweight. She frowned.

The pounding of footsteps on the stairs alerted Beth to the arrival of the children—at least Craig and Allie. They entered the room as though they had been in a race, with Craig winning. They both greeted her and plopped down on the couch, Allie giving the cushion several extra bounces.

"You're Jane's teacher. I've seen you at

church." Allie settled next to her brother, nudging him.

He poked his sister back. "She'll be down in a second. She's on the phone. Dad's making her get off."

Beth opened her mouth to interject something when Allie said, "She's in trouble. She called a friend long distance without telling Dad. She isn't supposed to. She didn't think Dad would find out, but he always does."

Beth clamped her lips together to keep from laughing. Samuel's children were a breath of fresh air. Jane probably didn't think so, but Beth did.

Samuel came back into the room with Jane following him, a sullen expression on her face, which looked so much like her beautiful mother's if only the young girl would smile. "Allie," he said in warning, giving her a stern look before heading toward the kitchen.

Jane mumbled something that sounded like hello and slouched into one of the maroon chairs, her legs sprawled out in front of her, crossed at the ankles. She glared at her little brother and sister.

"It's good to see you, Jane." Beth sat in the other maroon chair.

"Oh, I forgot you got a call earlier," Craig said to Jane.

"Who?"

"Some boy, I think."

Jane straightened, leaning forward, trying to appear nonchalant but not quite coming across that way. "You think? Who was it? You know you're not supposed to answer if you can't take a message."

Craig tapped his finger against his chin and rolled his eyes toward the ceiling. "Now, let me see. Bud. No. Brad. No."

"Dad!" Jane yelled.

Craig snapped his fingers. "I know. It was Sue."

"Sue! She's not a boy."

Craig grinned. "Yeah, I know."

"Dad!"

Samuel reentered the living room with Aunt Mae behind him. "We have a guest." He peered at each of his children, ending with Jane. "Remember your manners."

Listening to the children carry on brought back memories of when Beth had had all her siblings living at home. She had refereed many fights between them and knew exactly what Samuel had to deal with even though she had never been a parent. Those days were over with, had been for the past four years when her sister, Holly, had graduated and left her and Daniel for college.

"I need some help setting the table."

Beth started to offer, but Aunt Mae pointed to Allie and Craig. "Come on, you two. You need to earn your keep. Wash up before you get the plates."

After the children left, Aunt Mae said, "I'm glad you could join us this evening, Beth. I've heard so much about you. You do quite a bit around the church."

Beth absolutely hated compliments because she never knew what to do with them. If life were a stage production, her favorite place would be blending in with the scenery. "No more than others do."

"That's not what I hear. I know we're going to get along famously. Dinner's in ten minutes." Aunt Mae hurried back into the kitchen as a crash sounded.

Samuel skirted the chair Jane was in to sit on the couch across from his daughter. "I'm glad we have a few minutes alone. Jane, I wanted you to know I signed the papers today for you to be tested. Dr. Simpson said she would be calling you into her office over the next several weeks."

Jane's narrowed gaze flitted to Beth, then to her dad. "I can't miss class."

Samuel's eyes widened. "That's the first time you've ever said that. Dr. Simpson assures me she won't take you from your core classes."

"I don't want to miss drawing." Jane folded her arms over her chest.

Beth was going to break one of her rules and interfere in a family discussion. "Jane, this is important for you. Dr. Simpson may be able to help you. In my class you won't have to make up any work you miss while she's testing you. That's how strongly I feel about the testing."

Jane shot to her feet, her arms stiff at her sides. "Don't you two understand? I am not dumb! I will not be tested!" With tears glistening in her eyes, she stormed from the room.

Chapter Four

Samuel stared at the doorway where Jane had disappeared, a frown marring the perfection of his features. "That didn't go well."

"No," Beth answered, uncrossing then crossing her legs again.

He swung his gaze to hers. "Any suggestions?"

The vulnerability evident in Samuel called to her, and she couldn't resist it. "Let me talk to her. Give me a few minutes." She rose and started for the stairs.

"Jane's room is the first one on the left, and thanks."

She paused at the bottom of the steps and smiled back at him. "You're welcome, but I haven't done anything yet."

Relief lit his eyes. "I'm just glad you're

willing to try, because I've run out of things to do."

Beth made her way up the stairs, not quite sure what to say to Jane. *Lord, help me to approach her the right way. Help me to make her understand it's okay to ask for help, that we all have weaknesses we need to work on.*

At the closed door that Beth assumed was Jane's room, she stared at the dark wood, waiting for some kind of inspiration to strike. She had to reach the teenager or Jane would fail most of her classes.

She knew what it was like.

That was it! Beth had never talked to anyone about her struggles in school, but she was going to talk to Jane. Beth rapped several times on the door.

"Go away! I'm not hungry!" the teenager shouted from inside the room.

"Jane, it's Miss Coleman. May I have a word with you?" Beth clasped her hands together and rubbed her palms back and forth.

Silence stretched to two minutes. Then three.

Sighing, Beth started to leave.

The door swung open and Jane stood in the entrance. "I don't need to be tested."

"May I come in and talk to you?"

Jane hugged the door as if it held her up. "There's nothing you can say that will make me want to be tested."

"That may be true, but I still would like to talk to you." Beth moved toward Jane, and the teenager stepped out of the way and allowed Beth into her room.

Taking in the area before her, Beth noted the neat, organized items on the desk, dresser and bedside tables. No clothes were on the floor and even posters hung on the walls. A forest-green bedspread covered the made bed, which surprised Beth the most. It didn't look the room of any teenager she knew.

"You could give my brothers and sister lessons on keeping their rooms clean. Most of the time I never saw the floor in my youngest brother's bedroom. I think Daniel thought the floor was the trash can." Beth gestured toward the chair at the desk. "May I sit?"

"Sure." Jane shrugged and sat cross-legged on her bed, her hands grasping her knees.

After easing onto the hard-backed chair, Beth hesitated, not sure where to begin. It was part of her past she didn't dwell on. Looking at Jane, though, Beth knew that if it helped the young girl, then she had to tell her.

"Jane, when I was growing up, for years I

didn't know what was wrong with me. I struggled to read, and had to memorize every word. I couldn't sound out words like the other kids. My spelling was awful. Again, because I had to memorize everything. Thankfully I was determined to read, but it didn't come easily to me, especially when confronted with new words."

Jane averted her gaze, dropping her head and rubbing her hands down her jeans.

In her lap Beth laced her fingers, their tips turning red from her tight grip. "The day my mother decided to take me to a specialist to have me tested was the best day of my life. I finally got the help I needed. Of course, at the time I didn't think it was a good thing. I was angry at my mother. I didn't want the kids to think I was different, dumb. I even told my mom I wouldn't do what the lady asked me to do." Beth paused, waiting to see if Jane would say anything.

The teenager remained quiet with her head down, her hands continuing to rub her jeans.

Drawing in a fortifying breath, Beth offered up a silent prayer for help, then said, "The other students don't have to know you're being tested. This is between you and Dr. Simpson. No one else."

Jane finally lifted her head, tears shining in her eyes. "What if they want me to be in *those* classes?"

"Special education classes?"

Jane nodded.

"I don't see a need for that. You're very smart. You just need to learn some compensating skills. Once we find out why exactly you're having problems, then we can come up with ways to level the playing field for you in your classes. Make things a little easier for you."

A tear rolled down Jane's face. She scrubbed it away. "I don't want to be different."

"We're all different. Everyone has strengths and weaknesses. Every child in the school. Some can draw like you. Others can do math as well as you. You could probably tutor some of your classmates in math. Please let us try to help you."

Another tear, then another coursed down Jane's cheeks. "I'm not dumb. I know how to read."

"I never said you didn't. But when you write, you're struggling and it takes you a lot longer to read the passages. When I'm lecturing, you aren't taking notes. Why is that, Jane?"

The teenager bit down on her bottom lip

for a few seconds, then said, "Because I can't keep up with what you're saying. So what's the use?" Glaring at Beth, she uncrossed her legs and shoved herself to her feet. "Fine. Go ahead and test me."

Beth rose. "Remember, Jane, I have a master's degree in English and if I can do it, so can you. Anything is possible, but when you need help, you need to learn to accept it." Just as she had finally, with a great deal of patience from the lady who had tutored her during elementary and junior high school. She hoped Jane wasn't as stubborn as she had been.

"We'll see."

Beth headed for the door. "I bet dinner is ready by now. Are you coming down?" She took a deep breath of the air peppered with the scent of spices, bread and meat. "It sure smells wonderful."

"I guess so."

Jane followed Beth down the stairs. She felt the teenager's gaze on her the whole way to the living room where Samuel waited. His hopeful look greeted Beth and his daughter.

"Jane has agreed to the testing," Beth said, praying the girl didn't back out.

The teenager remained silent.

Relief washed over his features. "I'm glad, Jane." Samuel rose. "Aunt Mae says dinner is ready. I think Allie and Craig are already at the table, chomping at the bit to eat."

"They're always hungry," Jane muttered as she moved toward the dining room.

Beth started toward the room, too. Samuel reached out and stopped her with a hand on her arm. She glanced back, very aware that his touch did odd things to her pulse rate.

"How did you get her to agree?" he asked, his voice pitched low.

"I told her about my learning problem in school." It wasn't something she easily shared with others because of the painful memories of her struggles, but it felt right with Samuel—and Jane. Maybe her hardship while growing up would help the teenager cope with her own problem.

"Thank you. This is one father who is grateful for any help he can get."

"Dad, I'm starved. C'mon!"

Samuel chuckled. "Craig's always impatient."

Beth entered the dining room one step ahead of Samuel. A large oblong oak table with six chairs dominated the room. Four people, seated with napkins in their laps, looked expectantly at them.

"Daddy, can I say grace tonight?"

"Sure, Allie." Samuel pulled out the chair next to his at the head of the table and waited for Beth to be seated before scooting it forward.

When he took his place he bowed his head, which was Allie's signal to say, "God bless this food and help me to get invited to Sally Ann's party next weekend. Amen."

Beth smiled as she lifted her head.

"Who's Sally Ann?" Samuel asked, shaking out his cloth napkin and laying it in his lap.

"The most popular girl in my class. I've *got* to be invited!"

"We just moved here, honey. She may not have had a chance to get to know you yet."

"All the girls are getting invited. If I'm left out, no one will like me."

"Dad, can you pass the roast beef?" Craig asked, squirming around in his chair as though it were on fire.

Samuel looked down at the platter next to his plate and said, "Sorry." He took two slices of the meat and passed it to Beth, who was next to Craig. "Allie, they will like you. Just give them time to get to know you."

"If we didn't move around so much..." Jane let the rest of her sentence trail off into silence while she stared at her empty plate, ignoring the meat being passed around the table.

Samuel started the potatoes, then the carrots. "Hopefully that will change now that I'm out of the army, Jane."

"Good, Daddy. I'm tired of havin' to make new friends all the time." Allie scooped several potatoes onto her plate and only one small carrot.

Beth listened to the exchange at the table and remembered the days she'd had her sister and brothers at home and they had sat down to eat dinner. Some of their conversations had been lively. Now when she ate dinner the house was quiet. She often found herself with the radio on in the kitchen while she ate, because she still wasn't used to all that silence.

Jane filled her plate with the vegetables and said, "I have decided to become a vegetarian."

"Since when?" Aunt Mae asked, passing the rolls around the table.

"Since now. In biology today we saw a film on the meat packing industry. Yuck! You should have seen how—"

"I don't think we should discuss that at the table, Jane. We have a guest, remember?"

"I want to hear about it."

"Not now, Craig."

The firmness in Samuel's voice, accompanied by a frown on his face, emphasized the subject was to be dropped. Beth thought back to some of the topics her siblings had tried to discuss while eating. Thankfully she'd developed a stomach lined with iron.

For a good minute silence ruled at the table while everyone ate, their attention totally focused on their plates.

Beth took a bite of the roast beef, so tender she could cut it with her fork. "Mmm. Mae, this is delicious. Every year the women at church put out a recipe book in conjunction with the ladies' retreat. You should contribute this recipe."

"When do they do it?"

"In the fall. In fact, they'll need a person to put it together this year, since I'll be leaving and won't be able to." Beth hadn't thought about that job until she'd mentioned it to Mae. She really needed to sit down and make a list of the tasks she did at church and school and make sure someone else was lined up to do them.

Jane pinned her full attention on Beth. "You're leaving? When?"

The tone in Jane's voice chilled Beth. The expression on the teenager's face made Beth feel as though she had betrayed her. "Not until this summer. I'd never leave in the middle of the school year."

Some of the hostility evaporated as Jane looked away and picked at her potatoes with her fork. "Oh."

"I'm getting the impression you do a lot around the church." Samuel took a sip of his water.

"I like to be kept busy."

"As I've told Samuel before, working is good, but you also have to learn to play, too." Mae reached for another roll in the basket, sliced it and slathered butter on it.

"Yeah, I like to play," Craig chimed in.

"Me, too. Can I go play now, Daddy?" Allie hopped up.

Samuel lifted his hand, palm outward. "Hold it. We have company and not everyone is through with dinner yet."

Allie plopped back into the chair. "Sorry. I forgot."

"So what do you like to play with?" Beth asked, liking Samuel's youngest daughter, who was so full of energy. Beth wished she had half of it to help her get through a Friday night. Weariness nibbled at her, her shoulders aching, exhaustion stinging her eyes.

"Dolls. Daddy built me a playhouse and furniture for it. Do you want to see it?"

"I would love to, after dinner."

Allie grinned.

"How about you, Craig? What do you like to play with?"

"My Game Boy."

"My brother, Daniel, likes to do that, too."

"How old is he?"

"Nineteen. In the past few years, though, he doesn't play like he used to." Beth turned to Jane. "What do you like to do with your free time?"

She shrugged. "Listen to music. Draw."

"She drew me once. I have it up in my room. I can show you that, too." Allie gulped down the last of her milk.

"How about you, Beth?"

She looked toward Samuel and said, "Read whenever I get the chance. I've even started writing a bit. Short stories. That kind of thing."

"So you do have free time."

"Some. More now that my sister and brothers are gone." When she said the last sentence, something nagged at her. She should be celebrating that fact, but she wasn't. For years she had wanted more time for herself, and now she wasn't so sure that was really what she wanted. Maybe she was suffering from empty nest syndrome.

Samuel watched Beth stoop on the floor of Allie's bedroom and look inside the two-story Victorian dollhouse he had designed and built for his daughter over the previous year. It had been a kind of therapy for him and now that it was complete, he needed another project. He liked working with his hands. Maybe another dollhouse for the big Fourth of July auction the church always had for the outreach program.

"This is wonderful, Samuel. You're very talented."

"My daddy is the best." With her chin lifted at a proud angle, Allie stood next to Beth. "I helped Aunt Mae sew the curtains and bedspreads."

"You've thought of everything a home should have." Beth caressed the white cat curled by the fireplace with glowing logs in its grate. "Who painted the fireplace, the scenes out the windows?"

"Jane. Isn't she good?" Allie ran her finger across one large window that depicted a meadow scene with yellow, red and purple wildflowers growing abundantly in its field.

"Yes. I especially like her portrait of you over your bed." Gesturing toward the framed pen-and-ink picture of Allie that Jane had drawn, Beth pushed to her feet. "This was a family project, then?"

"Yeah, even Craig helped Daddy with sanding. He's learning to use Daddy's tools."

Beth turned to Samuel. "You have a workshop?"

"I did. I don't have one set up yet here."

"I imagine the basement could serve as a workshop. If I remember correctly, it's pretty big and only has the furnace and laundry room. They don't take up even half the space."

Samuel ran his hand through his hair, massaging the back of his neck. "I've been so busy I haven't really thought about setting up a workshop."

"You should. You're very good."

He felt his cheeks flame and was surprised at his reaction. Nothing usually threw him, but for some reason Beth's compliment had.

"I've thought about making a dollhouse for the annual auction."

"That would be great! Jesse and Darcy would love it."

"Aren't you the head of the auction?"

"Yes, but I'm turning the reins over to them. Remember, I'll be gone by then."

"Oh, yeah. I forgot." The thought of having only a few months to get to know Beth bothered him. He chalked it up to the fact she was an intricate part of the church and would be sorely missed when she left.

Beth heaved a deep sigh. "I'd better be going. It's been a long week and will be a busy weekend now that Daniel is home."

"I'll walk you to your car."

"You don't have to. I know the way."

"I know. I want to." Samuel fell into step beside Beth as they made their way down the stairs to the coat closet.

He helped Beth slip into her long black wool coat with a fake fur collar. After she fitted her hands into her black leather gloves, she made her way to the kitchen to tell Aunt Mae goodbye and thank her for the delicious dinner. When they walked back to the foyer, Samuel opened his front door, a blast of cold striking him in the face.

"Really, my car is right there in your driveway."

"Wait." Samuel snagged a jacket from a hanger and quickly donned it.

Outside on the porch a cold breeze swirled about them, making Samuel instinctively draw closer to Beth in an attempt to keep her warm. She didn't move away.

"I'm not a winter person. I'm really looking forward to spring."

He chuckled. "We have less than two months till the weather gets warmer."

Beth hurried down the steps toward her car. "Nothing beats spring. The colors are breathtaking after a drab winter. God sure knew what He was doing."

At her Jeep Samuel stopped her with a hand on her arm. "Do you think it will take long to get Jane tested?"

"I'll try to push it along."

"Why didn't I see this before now?"

"Jane has probably been very good at covering up her weaknesses."

"I should have been more aware of what was going on with Jane at school."

"When a child moves from school to school, she often gets lost in the shuffle."

His chest tightened, guilt gnawing at him.

"In other words, we shouldn't have moved so often."

"You didn't have a choice. That was your job."

"We always have a choice. I should have quit the army long before I did. But up until Ruth's death everything seemed fine. I can't believe I missed the signals. Ruth handled everything. I…" Samuel couldn't finish his sentence. His wife had kept the home running while he had kept the church running. It had worked, or at least until now he'd thought it had. What had he missed out on with his children? His guilt grew to knot his stomach.

"The important thing is that you're doing something about it now. Maybe I'm wrong and Jane is just rebelling."

"I don't know if I want you to be wrong or right."

Beth reached out and laid her hand over his on the car door. "Let's wait and see what the testing shows before we start throwing blame around. And even then, I strongly advise against blaming anyone or anything. It's wasted energy."

He smiled. "You're very wise, Beth Coleman. Have you thought about going into counseling?"

"I'll leave that job up to you. Teaching is what I love to do." She slid behind the steering wheel.

Samuel leaned into the car while she started it. "From what I've seen, you're very good at your job."

"And from what I've seen, you're very good at yours. The sermon last Sunday was inspiring."

He glanced away toward the streetlight that illuminated a part of his yard and the church. The building's gray stone facade mocked him. Its towering bell tower housing the brass bell that rang every Sunday jutted up toward heaven. In that moment he didn't feel worthy of setting foot in the church.

Guilt ridden, he stared at the dark shadows that surrounded the Garden of Serenity at the side of the building, where members of his congregation often found solace. In the dead of winter with snow still covering the ground he had walked its stone paths, sat on a wooden bench and looked at the pond, hoping for some kind of inspiration, and yet nothing had come to him. Instead, his sermon last Sunday had been a recycled one from when he had been in the army. He'd thought it had been an appropriate one right before

Lent, concerning Jesus' mission in the days preceding His death. More than anything he had needed to reconfirm why Christ had died for them.

"Are you all right?"

Samuel blinked, tearing his gaze away from the church. "Yes, I was just thinking about the garden."

"It won't be too long before we'll have to tend to it. Spring is around the corner." Beth started her car. "But even in winter I like to visit the garden from time to time. There's a certain beauty in the starkness of nature at this time of year. And with the pine trees and holly bushes it isn't totally brown."

"Is the garden's upkeep another one of your little projects around the church?"

Beth laughed. "No, I have a brown thumb when it comes to plants. Cooking's my forte. Joshua Markham is in charge of the garden."

"Good, because I have to confess I have a *black* thumb when it comes to gardening. I've been known to kill a cactus because I under-watered it. I have to admit I can't cook, either."

"But you do beautiful things with your hands. I mean…"

Samuel heard the flustered tone in Beth's voice, but couldn't make out her features. He could imagine a blush tainting her cheeks. She blushed so easily, but the red tinge added a glow to her face, enhancing her beauty. "I know what you mean. God gives us each a talent."

"Yes, and we need to emphasize that to Jane."

"I've tried. But for some reason she doesn't think my opinion counts. She once told me I have to love her because I'm her father."

Beth sighed. "I wish that were true."

A touch of pain laced her words as though Beth knew firsthand the falseness of that conception. In a perfect world all parents would love their children and there would be no mental or physical abuse. He knew from counseling parishioners that wasn't true. Was Beth's knowledge derived from being a teacher or from personal experience? He remembered her telling him about her father leaving her mother. He shivered, thinking of the answer to that question.

Beth reached over and switched on her heater. "I'd better go before you freeze."

Samuel watched her disappear down the

street, suddenly wishing that the evening wasn't over. Her caring nature added a charm to Beth Coleman that was very appealing. That observation took him by surprise. He hadn't thought of a woman being appealing since the death of his wife, his high school sweetheart, the only person he'd ever seriously dated.

"Then if we all are in agreement, we'll put Jane on an individual education plan where she can utilize these modifications we have discussed to help her with her auditory processing problem." Dr. Simpson, the school psychologist, shuffled some papers and produced a sheet of paper, which she signed then slid across the table to Samuel. "If you'll sign here, saying that she qualifies for special education services under the category of learning disabilities, Ms. Jones will go over the IEP."

Beth noticed Jane pale and ball her hands in her lap when Nancy Simpson said "learning disabilities." The teenager's teeth dug into her lower lip. Beth's heart wrenched at the sight of the child fighting back tears.

"Jane, you should sign, too." Dr. Simpson guided the paper toward her after Samuel had penned his name.

Jane stared at the paper on the table before her. She started to say something, but her lower lip trembled. She dropped her head, her shoulders hunched over.

Sitting next to the teenager, Beth covered Jane's hand with hers. "No one needs to know you are on an IEP unless you choose to tell. This is kept strictly confidential."

"Everyone will know. They'll think I'm dumb."

The waver in the teenager's voice tightened a band about Beth's chest. She knew exactly how Jane felt. She realized Jane would have to come to terms with her disability in order to get the help she needed. That wasn't easy when she was a fifteen-year-old in a new school. Jane should have a circle of friends much as Darcy, Jesse, Zoey, Tanya and she had. Then maybe the teenage girl wouldn't feel so alone.

"It won't come from us, Jane. No one will know you'll have a copy of the teacher's notes. No one will know you have extended time for your tests. All these accommodations can be carried out without others knowing."

Jane's head jerked up, and she glared at each person sitting at the table. Tears shone in her eyes. She shoved back her chair and shot out of it. "I won't sign the paper." She rushed for the door.

Chapter Five

Samuel's gaze snagged Beth's across the empty chair between them. A dazed expression in his eyes told of his own overwhelming feelings concerning the past thirty minutes. A myriad of tests and their scores had been thrown at him, along with a list of recommendations to help Jane. He might have thought he had been prepared, but from his look Beth doubted he really had been.

Beth rose. "Let me see if I can explain again that everything will be kept private." She directed her statement to Samuel, who nodded.

She left the conference room and went in search of Jane. Beth's black pumps clicked against the tile floor, echoing in the empty hall, as she walked toward her room. Jane had probably escaped outside; she was maybe even at her father's car waiting for him at this very moment. Beth decided to grab her coat and check the parking lot. The cold chill of a late February afternoon would go right through her if she didn't.

She stepped into her classroom and halted. Jane stood at the window, her shoulders sagging forward, her chin resting on her chest, her head touching the cold pane.

"I'm not going back in there, Miss Coleman." Jane drew in a huge breath and held it for a few extra seconds. "I saw how everyone was looking at me. I don't need anyone's help. If I want to do good in school, I will."

Beth covered the space between them, stopping a few feet from Jane. "I've looked at your records from your previous schools. I know you can do well in school. Up until a few years ago your grades were good. I noticed you had some trouble in elementary school, especially with reading, but you seemed to overcome that."

Jane spun about and took a step back. "So you're wondering what happened. I don't care anymore about school. I'm—I'm..." Tears slipped from her eyes and rolled down her cheeks. As quickly as she wiped them away, more appeared.

Beth moved closer. "I know when I reached high school I started to have more trouble. The work was harder, so therefore it took longer to do my homework and assignments, to memorize what I needed to know, to read the work I needed to do. Is that what's happening?"

Jane kept her gaze turned away, but nodded.

"Some of the things we're suggesting to help you will make it easier for you. Hopefully you won't feel so overwhelmed."

Jane squared her shoulders and looked Beth in the eye. "I'm not overwhelmed. I don't care anymore."

"Why don't you?"

Her bottom lip began to tremble. Jane bit into it and looked away.

Determined to discover what was behind Jane's statement, Beth stepped even closer and laid a hand on the teenager's shoulder. "Why, Jane?"

"My grades…"

Beth moved into Jane's direct line of vision. She lifted the young girl's chin. "I care, Jane."

"My grades were important—" Jane swallowed hard "—to my mom. She helped me study when I was having trouble."

"You didn't care about having good grades?"

"No." With a sheen to her eyes Jane stared at Beth. "Yes, I wanted good grades, too."

"But that changed when your mom died?"

Jane wrenched away from Beth and crossed her arms over her chest. "Everything changed when my mom died."

Her palms sweaty, Beth curled her hands into tight fists. With a conscious effort she tried to relax against the radiator as though the conversation they were having was mundane, unimportant. "You know, Jane, you and I are a lot alike."

Jane leaned back against the other end of the radiator. "How so?"

The girl's tone of voice spoke of her doubts that a teacher and she would be alike in any way. Beth suppressed a grin and said, "I lost my mother when I was nineteen. She was my world, and when she died I didn't know what to do. There are times I still think about her and my heart breaks even after all these years."

Jane slanted a look toward her. "You do?"

"But she's always in here." Beth touched her heart. "No one can take that away from me." She ran her hand along the radiator, feeling its heat chase away the chills the memories brought. "If you want, I'll tutor you at your house. No one will need to know. It'll be between you and me. We can do it several times a week in the evening. What do you say?"

"Why would you do that?"

"Because I care what happens to you. Jane, I think you're very smart and have a lot of potential. I don't want to see you throw it away. Will you let me help you?"

"I still don't want to sign the papers."

"I know. The accommodations will be there for you to utilize if you choose to. It's not easy asking for help. I know. I've been in your shoes."

Someone cleared his throat. Beth looked toward the doorway at the same time as Jane. Samuel stood just a foot inside the room. How much had he heard? Beth wondered, and pushed herself away from the radiator. "Is the meeting over?"

"Yes. Are you ready to go home, Jane?"

"You mean I don't have to go back and sign the papers?"

"Not if you don't want to."

She straightened, her chin tilted at a proud angle. "I don't. I'm going to my locker and get my books."

When Jane left, the silence in the room grew. Beth wanted to ask if Samuel had overheard any of their conversation, but couldn't find the words. She made her way to her desk to gather up her papers. "I've offered to help Jane in the evening a couple of times a week. Is that all right with you?"

"Where?"

"Your house. She doesn't want anyone to find out."

"Do you have that kind of time?"

Beth swung her gaze to Samuel's. "I do for her. This is something I want to do, unless you object."

"No! I'm thrilled she has agreed. Maybe you can reach her. No one else has been able to since her mother died."

The touch of vulnerability always just below Samuel's surface emerged. It was obvious that his wife's death had deeply affected more than Jane. He was floundering just as much as his daughter. Could she help both father and daughter? Would she be able to before she left Sweetwater?

Lord, give me the knowledge and strength to know what to do to help both of them. They are lost and need Your love and guidance.

When Jane finished explaining the functions of each branch of government, Beth said, "I think you're ready for your government test tomorrow. What do you think?"

Jane raised one shoulder in a shrug. "I guess so."

"Did it help to have a copy of the teacher's lecture notes?"

Jane turned her head away, doodling on the piece of paper in front of her. "Yeah," she murmured in such a low voice Beth wouldn't have heard her if she hadn't been sitting right next to her at the table.

"Good. Then I'll continue to get your teachers' notes for you." Beth hoped one day that Jane would begin to ask for the notes on her own, but until then she would. Jane needed to be convinced the accommodation worked for her.

Beth knew the second Samuel appeared in the dining-room doorway. She felt the power of his gaze and met it with a smile that lightened her heart. For the past month she had been coming to his house to tutor Jane three times a week, and every time she was about to leave he would appear and they would end up talking. At first about Jane. Now their conversation covered just about every topic in the news—but nothing really personal and certainly nothing about his deceased wife. Beth wasn't sure how she could help him when he wouldn't let her in.

"Jane, there's a call for you. You can get it in my office."

Jane furrowed her brow. "I can pick up in the kitchen."

"You might want to take this call in my office."

The teenager pushed herself to her feet, dropping the pencil she had been doodling with onto the open notebook. "Who is it?"

"A boy."

"It is?" The perplexed look on Jane's face deepened as she headed toward her father's office, her steps quickening.

"Are you two through for the evening?" Samuel came into the room and stood on the other side of the table.

"Yes." Beth gathered her books and papers and stuffed them into her briefcase. "A boy calling Jane. I wonder who it is."

"I was sorely tempted to ask his name, but

I suspect Jane wouldn't be too thrilled if I did. But you can bet I will be asking my daughter when she is through talking to the young man. I'm a firm believer in knowing what is going on in my children's lives. And this latest problem with Jane at school tells me I have been neglecting that responsibility. I won't do that again."

"Don't be so hard on yourself. Kids can be great at hiding things, and with you all moving so much the previous schools didn't pick up on Jane's problems, either. Sadly, that happens."

"But after only a few weeks, you saw something." Samuel skirted the table and took her briefcase from her to carry to her car.

"It's because Jane reminds me of myself at her age."

"You mentioned something about that before. You had the same kind of problems in school as my daughter?" He started for the foyer.

"Yes. I struggled for years. Actually I still do. I changed to trying to learn Portuguese on tape, but I'm not doing as well as I'd hoped. I have a hard time hearing the different sounds. I'm hoping when I live in a country it will come faster to me."

"I didn't know."

"Not many people do. I don't broadcast my difficulties, just as Jane doesn't. Here I am a perfectly intelligent woman and I can't seem to learn a foreign language. It's not something I want everyone to know, so I guess we all have our secrets."

"But you shared yours with me."

"To help you to understand Jane better and why she kept so much to herself and didn't ask you for help. Haven't you had a problem you haven't asked another soul for help with?"

The frown that touched his features, his look that sliced away told Beth the answer to that question. He had his secrets, too.

Samuel busied himself by retrieving Beth's wool coat from the closet. He helped her to slip into the garment, then reached around to open the front door. "Are you sure I can't pay you for your tutoring?"

"No. We've been through this before, Samuel. I don't want your money. I'm doing this for Jane."

"Then at least let me take you out for dinner."

"I don't—"

"Please, Beth. Do this for me. I feel like I should do something for you."

She paused on the porch, looking back at Samuel framed in the doorway with the light behind him and his features in the shadows. Dinner? Like a real date? The reason she hadn't pushed him to speak about his personal life, even though she needed to know details to help him, was that she had felt it would be a mistake. The more she found out about Samuel, the more she liked him and he didn't fit into her future plans at all, especially with his ready-made family. Besides, how could she compare to his high school sweetheart, whom he had loved so much that his grief had thrown his life into turmoil, as a few of his comments had indicated?

"You don't have to do a thing. But if it's important to you, I'll go to dinner with you." The second she agreed to go out with him, a damp layer of perspiration coated her face even though it was chilly outside.

A date! What would she wear? What would they talk about? They had already exhausted every topic concerning current events. She needed help.

"Great. How about Saturday night? We could go to dinner and a movie. I'll pick you up at seven—and wear something nice."

"Okay. Where are we going?"

"It's a surprise."

"But—"

"No, Beth, I'm not going to tell you, but it will be a special place. That is the least I can do for you."

A surprise? She wasn't good with surprises, but the firm line of his jaw told her no amount of pleading would get the name of the restaurant out of him. She reached for her briefcase. "I can find my way to my car. Stay inside where it's warm."

When her hand clasped the handle, his brushed across her knuckles, sending sparks up her arm. She snatched her briefcase and spun about, hurrying down the steps. He remained in the doorway, watching her retreat. Not until she had backed out of his driveway did he close the front door.

Her hand shook on the steering wheel and a thin layer of perspiration still covered her face. It was way too hot in her car, and she didn't even have the heater on. She should have removed her coat before climbing into the Jeep.

The minute she arrived at her house, she rushed to the phone and called Jesse. "Help! I have a date."

* * *

"Okay. This isn't the end of the world, Beth. Zoey and I will help you find something to wear." Jesse opened the door to a chic dress shop along Main Street.

"I love to shop for clothes. This will be fun." Zoey followed Beth into the store, bringing up the rear.

"It may be fun for you two, but not for me. I don't like to shop." Beth scanned the racks and racks of clothing and hated the thought of trying on one dress after another. It had always made her feel so fat. "I'm not easy to fit. If it's right on the top, it isn't on the bottom."

"We all have something to contend with. I have a hard time finding clothes short enough. Not every place carries petite." Zoey went straight for the after-five dresses and began looking through them.

Jesse checked out the nice pantsuits, while Beth stood in the middle of the store, probably looking lost if the expression on the saleswoman's face was any indication.

She hurried over to Beth. "May I be of help?"

"I'm just browsing."

Zoey turned toward the saleswoman. "She

needs a special dress for a dinner date to a nice restaurant. Any suggestions?"

The older woman stepped back and allowed her gaze to trek down Beth's length. When she reestablished eye contact with Beth, she said, "I have a black number that would look great on you. We just received it and it's still in the back. Let me get it for you."

Zoey came to stand beside Beth while Jesse continued to look. "Black would look good on you."

"But I always wear black and gray. I need something different. Isn't that the object of this shopping trip? I have several nice black dresses at home." Because she'd heard once that black was slimming, she added silently.

"There are times black is appropriate. I've seen your black dresses and they aren't nice enough. Too practical. For a dinner at a nice restaurant black can be just right."

"With the right touches," Jesse added, throwing them a glance over her shoulder.

When the saleswoman walked out holding a short black dress on a hanger, its soft folds falling in a graceful pattern, Beth knew it was perfect for her—if only it fit. She took it from the older woman and headed for the dressing room. After slipping the black outfit over her head, she faced the mirror while struggling with the zipper in back. Zipping it up, she assessed herself. For once she believed that black was a slimming color.

The silk material fell in soft folds to below her knees, disguising her thighs. She immediately thought of the black shoes she had worn to her party at the end of January. They would be perfect with the dress. Its scooped neckline and thin spaghetti straps screamed for something around her neck, though. She thought of her limited jewelry and wasn't sure what she would wear to complement the outfit.

When she stepped out of the dressing room, she found both Zoey and Jesse waiting. In Zoey's hand was a red feather boa.

She handed it to Beth. "This will be perfect with it. Drape it around your neck."

Beth waved her hand toward the red boa. "I can't wear that!"

"Yes, you can. You wanted something different. This is different." Zoey draped it around Beth's neck, then moved back to evaluate the outfit. "This will knock his socks off."

Beth's eyes grew wide. "I don't want to knock our minister's socks off."

"Why not? He's single and eligible. You're single and eligible. Perfect." Jesse slowly circled her with her finger against her chin. "Yes, I believe, Zoey, that's the perfect touch."

"What was I thinking, bringing you two to help me shop for something to wear?"

"That we have good taste and won't steer you in the wrong direction." Zoey turned Beth around and gently pushed her toward the dressing room. "She'll take all of it," she said to the saleswoman.

"Next we need to visit my hair salon," Jesse called out as Beth disappeared into the room.

Beth rolled her eyes and wondered what had come over her when she had called Jesse for help. Insanity, she decided as she donned her gray wool pantsuit with its white long-sleeved shirt. Red! She never wore red!

The doorbell rang promptly at seven. Running her hand through her new shorter hair that framed her face and fell to just below her chin in soft curls, Beth took one last look at herself in the mirror and drew in a deep, cleansing breath as though that would fortify her for the rest of the evening. Why hadn't she dated more? The answer was that for so many years she had been wrapped up in raising a family and she hadn't had much time. Then most of the men she'd known had become unavailable and the available ones she'd known too well to want to date them. Now her inexperience left her a nervous wreck. Would her stomach ever stop roiling long enough for her to enjoy the dinner?

Beth quickly made her way to the foyer, checked to see if it was Samuel, then opened the front door. "Come in. I need to get my wrap. Is it cold outside?"

Samuel's face lit with a smile as his gaze took in her attire. "Actually we have a breeze from the south and it's not too bad for March."

Backing toward the coat closet, Beth noted that Samuel was wearing a dark gray suit with a red tie. She fingered the red boa draped around her neck and hanging down her front. His gaze was riveted to her hand on it.

"I like that," he said, his voice low.

Its sound slipped down the length of her, warming every inch. Both of them had worn something red. She felt a kinship with him that surprised her, as though the color bonded them, when it really was something else—intangible, undefinable. With her gaze connected to his, Beth fumbled for her black coat with its fur collar.

Samuel stepped forward. "Here, let me get it for you." He reached around her, his arm brushing against hers, and snatched her coat off its hanger.

As he held it for her, Beth murmured, "Thank you." She was aware of him behind her, his breath fanning her neck. Her eyes slid closed and she breathed in his distinctive aftershave.

"You're beautiful tonight," he whispered close to her ear.

For the first time she actually felt beautiful. She knew she really wasn't, but his words touched her deeply, causing her pulse to race. She could not remember having a male say those words to her except her brothers when they had been young boys or when they had been trying to get something from her.

"Jesse and Zoey went shopping with me. Actually they insisted I go shopping with them and wouldn't take no for an answer."

"Who thought of this red boa?"

"Zoey. She loves red and gravitates toward anything red in a store." Beth gestured toward his tie. "Who picked out your red tie?"

A cloud descended over his expression. "My wife. Red was her favorite color."

"Oh" was all Beth could manage to say, heat suffusing her face. Her cheeks must rival her red boa, she thought.

The smile that graced Samuel's mouth seemed forced as he asked, "What is your favorite color?"

Beth grinned, not wanting the evening to start off awkwardly. "Yellow. I think some people probably think it's black or gray, because that's what I wear a lot, but I love what yellow represents—sunshine."

"Mine is green and I have no reason for liking it except that I've always felt that way since I was a little boy."

Beth moved toward the front door. "Are you going to tell me where we're going to eat dinner now?"

"Nope. It's a surprise. You'll know when we pull up to the restaurant."

"You know I don't like surprises."

"I'm still not going to tell you. I like to surprise people." Samuel pulled the door closed behind him and made sure it was locked before guiding Beth toward his Mustang, which was parked in her drive.

As Samuel backed out onto the street, Beth still felt the impression of his fingers at the small of her back as he'd led her to his car. Her excitement grew as she thought of all the places they could be going. She rarely went out to eat except to a fast-food restaurant or Alice's Café. It had to be a very nice restaurant, since he wanted her to dress up— which excluded those places and most of the other ones in Sweetwater.

When he drove into the parking lot at the side of the best, most expensive restaurant in the county, she was at a loss for words. In all her years in Sweetwater she had never set foot inside, because she couldn't afford to eat at the place. That hadn't stopped her from dreaming about having dinner at Andre's.

"I think you've made a mistake," she said, turning slightly to face him in the car.

"A mistake?"

"Andre's is very expensive."

"I know. You won't accept money for tutoring Jane, so this is the next best thing. I want to show you how much I appreciate all the time you've spent working with my daughter."

"But—"

He pressed his fingers to her lips. "No buts, Beth. This evening is all about you."

The feel of his touch melted any reservations she had. How could she refuse?

When he escorted her into the restaurant she scanned the dimly lit room with elegantly set tables, the crystal and china gleaming in the candlelight. An arrangement of white roses adorned each table and gold utensils picked up the gold in the cream-colored china. She'd never seen anything so richly decorated except in a magazine.

After they were shown to a table set in an alcove, secluded and private, Beth opened her menu to find no prices were listed. She knew she was in trouble then. She had planned on ordering the cheapest item on the menu, but that was hard to figure out.

"Don't worry about the cost, Beth."

"But I'm on the budget committee and I know how much you make as our minister."

"Don't worry. I wouldn't have brought you here if I couldn't afford it. This won't cost me what it would have cost to hire a tutor for Jane." He laid his hand over hers on the white linen tablecloth and captured her gaze within his. "Besides, Beth, you deserve the best.

You do so much for everyone else that it's about time someone did something for you."

Heat scorched her cheeks. Compliments always made her feel uneasy. She looked away and caught sight of Nick and Jesse sitting across the room from them. Her friend waved, a huge grin on her face. Suspicion began to dawn in Beth's mind.

"Did anyone suggest this restaurant to you?"

Samuel chuckled. "I got some help from one of my parishioners."

That would be the last time she confided in Jesse. Beth returned her friend's greeting with a narrowed gaze. "Jesse Blackburn?"

"Actually her husband, Nick."

"Nick!"

"I figured a man of his means would know the best place to eat in a fifty-mile radius."

"So Jesse didn't tell you I've always dreamed of having dinner at Andre's?"

One corner of his mouth hitched in a lop-sided grin. "No, but thanks for letting me know my choice was a good one. It isn't every day a guy can make a lady's dream come true."

The appreciative gleam in his eyes, coupled with his heart-melting smile, sent her heartbeat racing. She dropped her gaze to the elaborate gold-and-cream china, his hand continuing to cover hers. Warmth crackled at the contact.

"What other dreams do you have, Beth Coleman? I know about traveling and seeing the world, and now this one. But surely you have others."

Her lungs expanded as she drew in a deep breath and held it for a few extra seconds. "Actually, I don't. Of course, I want my brothers and sister to do well."

His forehead creased. "Nothing else? No fame, fortune?"

"I'm a very simple person. I don't require a lot to be happy."

Samuel glanced beyond her right shoulder. "Hold that thought. I think our waiter is waiting for us to order." He slid his hand back and picked up the menu to study.

She missed his touch the second it was gone, and that realization surprised her. She had always been sensible, never particularly getting all weak-kneed over any movie star or celebrity everyone else was raving about. Quickly she lifted her menu to peruse before she did something foolish like put her hand over his. After narrowing the choices to filet mignon and pork, she went with the roast pork with a crab stuffing, corn creamed mashed potatoes and steamed vegetables.

After the waiter took their orders, Beth leaned forward and asked, "What is one of your dreams? It's not fair for you to know two of mine and I don't know one of yours."

"Beth, haven't you heard life isn't fair?"

"Yes, and I won't accept that answer. Evading my question isn't an option."

He tapped his finger against his chin and looked toward the ceiling as though in deep thought. "Mmm. Let me see. What is a dream I've had?"

"No, what is a dream you have now?"

His eyes darkened, a somber expression descending. "To keep my family together."

She shook her head. "Your family is together."

"Not together so much as back to the way it once was before…" His words faded into silence.

"Before your wife died?"

He nodded.

"What happened?"

He opened his mouth to say something, but clamped it shut and stared off to the side of Beth. When he reestablished eye contact with her, he said, "I wasn't there for Ruth when she needed me the most. I couldn't help her. I had to watch her die from breast cancer and I could do nothing to take the pain away." He swallowed hard. "One of the last things she said to me was that she regretted most not being able to have another child with me. We'd both wanted another and had been trying for months. Then she died and I couldn't even deal with the three children I had. I was too busy grieving, questioning God for taking her from me."

The pain in his voice underscored the depth of the despair he had sunk to after his wife's death. Tears choked off her words, making it difficult to respond to him.

He pinned her with his intense gaze. "I haven't told anyone else this. I don't even know why I told you. I shouldn't have."

She reached toward him. "I'm glad you did." She suppressed her own reeling emotions to help him. "We can't go back, Samuel. You know that. We have to make a new future with what God has given us."

He clenched his jaw. "That's easy for you to say. You're looking toward your future with anticipation. You'll be leaving in a few months to fulfill one of your dreams."

"And haven't you come to Sweetwater to start a new future for you and your family?"

"Yes, but—"

"No, there aren't any buts. This is a good place to forge a new beginning. Craig and Allie seem to be a part of this town already, and I believe Jane will be soon. She's fighting it, but she is the oldest. I think a boy in one of my classes, Ryan, likes Jane. She said something about him calling her a couple of times. That's a good start."

"Yes, but—"

The waiter chose that moment to bring their salads. Samuel clamped his mouth closed in a tight, thin line while the young man placed the small plates in front of them. Beth drenched her greens with a honey mustard dressing, aware of the strained silence between her and Samuel.

When the waiter was gone, Samuel continued. "But we're not the family we once were."

"Of course not." Beth stabbed a piece of spinach with her fork and brought it to her mouth. "Your children are growing up. Their needs will be different. Even your needs will change with time."

"My needs aren't important at the moment."

"You can't neglect them, Samuel. As the head of the family, you set its tone."

His hand on his fork paused above his salad. His knuckles whitened, his jaw hard. "How did we get on such a heavy topic of conversation?"

Beth took a swallow of ice water. "I hope the weatherman is wrong about another big snow in a few days."

Tension siphoned from his expression, and he chuckled. "I didn't mean we had to resort to talking about the weather."

Beth placed her fork on her nearly empty salad plate. "What do you want to talk about? It's your call."

"This is your evening." He finished the last bite of his salad. "How's your brother doing in college?"

"I haven't heard from him in a couple of weeks, and he hasn't paid me any more surprise visits just so I could do his laundry. I took your advice and told him he would have to learn to do his own clothes and that I would be glad to give him lessons. I guess he believed me."

"Good. He'll thank you one day," Samuel said as the waiter removed the salad plates and served them their entrées.

"I hope so. He wasn't too happy when I told him."

"Aunt Mae is already teaching Craig what to do, and since Craig is learning, Allie wants to do hers."

"How about Jane?"

"Complains the whole time, but she does it." He looked down at his sirloin steak, drenched in a butter sauce. "I have to admit that I wasn't the one who insisted the children learn to do their own laundry. It was Aunt Mae. She whipped our household into shape."

"She's doing a good job at the church, too. She has volunteered to help Tanya with the Sunday-school program and she's helping Jesse and Zoey with the auction, not to mention taking over producing the recipe book."

"I thought Darcy was going to be on the committee to help with the auction."

"Darcy will help some, but with having a baby any day now, we all thought it might be better if Zoey is the other cochairwoman."

"Let's see, what other jobs do I need to find a replacement for before you leave?" Samuel held up his hand and ticked them off. "One, the budget committee, two, the ladies' retreat in the fall and…" he frowned. "I'm forgetting something."

"The bookstore."

He shook his head. "What are we going to do without you?"

She cut a piece of her pork. "Carry on."

"I'm not so sure about that, Beth. You're an important part of the church."

Suddenly she wished she was an important part of his life, and that thought shocked her. She nearly choked on the piece of meat she was chewing and had to gulp down some water. She had no business even thinking something like that. He still loved Ruth, still wore his wedding ring, had pictures of her all over his house. How could she compete with his beautiful, deceased wife? Besides, she had her own life planned—had planned for years—what she was going to do when her sister and brothers finally left their childhood home.

"Nick would be perfect for the budget committee, and by fall I think Darcy would be able to help with the ladies' retreat. Her baby will be six months old by then."

"And the bookstore?"

"Check with Felicia. She's the town librarian. She loves books and cats."

"On top of everything else, you know everyone so well. You're a fountain of information and I've come to rely on you for advice on more than how to deal with my daughter."

She'd thought her cheeks had reddened before, but nothing like they were now. She was afraid if she touched them, her fingertips would be burned.

"Your absence will leave a gaping hole in this town."

Beth held up her hand. "Stop. No more compliments. I won't know what to do if you continue."

He bent forward, again placing his hand over hers. "That's your problem. You don't know your own value to the people in Sweet-water."

Speechless, she stared into his eyes. So intent was she on Samuel, she jumped when someone stopped next to her. She slipped her hand free and brought it up to cover her heart. "Jesse, you scared me."

"Sorry about that."

Beth could tell by the impish expression on her friend's face she wasn't sorry one bit.

"I wanted to tell you before we headed out that Joshua called to tell me he was at the hospital. Darcy is in labor and should have the baby soon, according to the doctor. I told him I would let you know."

Chapter Six

"Darcy's having her baby?" Beth shot to her feet, her napkin floating to the floor. "We've got to go. I mean…" Her hand fluttered in the air.

Jesse pressed her down into her chair. "Finish eating your dinner. It will still be a while and it isn't every day you eat at Andre's. You know Darcy wouldn't be too happy with you if you cut your date short."

"We'll be along as soon as we eat." Samuel picked up Beth's napkin and gave it to her, amused by her flustered expression. "Thanks for telling us."

Beth began eating fast.

"You certainly are excited for Darcy, but you might actually want to chew your food and taste it."

Beth stopped for a few seconds, then swallowed slowly what she had in her mouth. "She's one of my best friends and she's wanted this baby so much. I think I've been through this pregnancy with her."

"Right about now she's probably wishing you were the one delivering the baby."

"I don't doubt that, but I'm glad I'm not the one having a baby."

"You don't want any children? You're so good with them."

"I'm no spring chick," she said with a gleam dancing in her eyes.

He nearly spewed out the water he was drinking. "Spring chick! You're only thirty-eight. That isn't over the hill. You're not even near the top. Please, no more talk of how old you are."

Beth forked the last of the steamed broccoli. "I have already raised three children. I've never been on my own and not had children to take care of." She slid the utensil into her mouth and took her time chewing.

To Samuel, Beth was the perfect mother, so her declaration surprised him, and yet he understood. Most nineteen-year-olds didn't have to raise three siblings all at once. Beth had, and from all he had heard from the people at church, she had done an excellent job. She deserved some time to do what she wanted.

"But that doesn't mean I won't help Darcy out with baby-sitting. I don't think she'll have trouble getting any of us to help her. Zoey, Jesse, Tanya and I will be fighting over it in no time."

After Samuel paid the bill, he pulled out Beth's chair and escorted her from the restaurant. The whole way to the hospital she tapped her fingers against the door handle as though that would speed things up.

As he neared the hospital, he slanted a look at Beth. He and Ruth had wanted more children. He still did. He tried to picture Beth with child. The image came easily to his mind. She would be a good mother. Her loving, caring way was such a natural part of her. Any child she raised would be lucky. And thirty-eight wasn't too old to have a baby!

Baby? Children? He put a halt to the direction his thoughts were going in. That wasn't in his future. He was still trying to handle the family he already had.

Samuel pulled into a parking space near the front door of the three-story hospital. He climbed from the car, intending to go around and open Beth's door. She exited more quickly than he did and hurriedly made her way to the sliding glass doors. Chuckling, especially when he thought of her comment earlier about not being a spring chick, he entered the building a few paces behind her. Beth Coleman exhibited a youthful spring to her step.

She stopped at the reception desk to ask about Darcy. Watching her talk to the woman behind the desk, Samuel noted Beth's flushed cheeks, the smile that brightened her whole face and a liveliness that gave her a fresh, wholesome look. He knew she discounted her appearance as being plain, unappealing, but she didn't see herself through his eyes. She was full of energy and enthusiasm that made her very appealing. He didn't understand why some man hadn't snapped her up.

Beth turned to him, her eyes twinkling with excitement. "Darcy's in the delivery room right now. It won't be long. Let's go to the waiting room. That's where everyone else is."

"Beth Coleman, I should have known you wouldn't be more than a few steps behind us getting here," Jesse said as Beth and Samuel entered the waiting room.

Samuel scanned the faces of his parishioners—a roomful of them, all here because of Darcy Mark-ham. If it had been announced on the news, he wouldn't have been surprised to find half the town waiting to hear about the new baby. That was the way Sweetwater was. The town took care of its own. He was counting on that, because he needed to feel as though he belonged somewhere. He needed to reconnect with God and why he had become a minister in the first place. If not—he shuddered to think of what he would have to do if he didn't.

"You didn't think you would drop that bomb on me and I would cheerfully go on eating as though nothing was happening." Beth hugged Jesse, then Zoey and Tanya.

"You finished your meal, didn't you?" Jesse asked, stepping back against her husband, who brought his arms around her.

"Yes, but I'm not sure what I ate after you left."

Jesse captured Samuel's attention. "I'm sorry about that. I stayed away as long as I could, but I couldn't wait any longer."

Nick laughed. "You can say that again. I had to practically hog-tie her to keep her in her chair after the phone call from Joshua.

She wanted to run right over that very second and announce the news to you two. Fifteen minutes was all I could persuade her to be quiet and let you eat in peace."

Jesse placed one hand on her waist. "Honestly, Beth, I've never seen you eat so slowly before."

"I wish I could have seen that," Zoey said, taking her chair again between Tanya and Darcy's father.

"Why's it taking so long?" Darcy's dad asked, his brows coming together.

Liz, his new wife, took his hand and patted it. "Babies come in their own time."

"You can say that again. With my last one I barely got to the hospital, but with my oldest I was in labor for over a day."

Having made a point of finding out about his parishioners, Samuel noticed the faraway look that appeared in Zoey's eyes as she spoke, and he realized she was thinking back to the birth of her baby daughter, a birth she'd had to go through without her husband because he was missing in action while on assignment for the DEA. He could imagine the pain she had gone through—pain that had nothing to do with delivering a baby—because he'd gone through the same kind of pain when he'd lost Ruth to breast cancer.

"Thankfully the doctor doesn't think it will be a day." Jesse plopped down across from Sean, Darcy's son. "Are you excited, kiddo?"

He nodded, but his eyelids were drooping. Liz drew him against her and rested his head against her shoulder.

At that moment Joshua came into the waiting room and everyone turned their attention toward him. "It's a little girl. She's seven pounds, eight ounces and has a great set of lungs. The doctor says she is one healthy baby."

Relief mixed with thankfulness flowed through Samuel as the room filled with everyone talking at once. He raised his hands, palms outward, and said, "I think this would be a good time to say a prayer."

"Oh, yes, let's join hands." Zoey stood and stretched out her arms on both sides of her.

With hands clasped together, Darcy's friends and family stood in a circle with their heads bowed.

Expected to lead the prayer, Samuel took a deep, cleansing breath and said, "Heavenly Father, please watch out for this newest addition to the Markham family and Sweetwater

Community Church. Help us to guide her in Your ways and to bring her into Your fold. Amen."

There were a few seconds of silence then voices erupted with questions, all directed at an exhausted-looking Joshua.

"When can we see her? What is her name?" Beth asked, shifting from one foot to the other.

Joshua gave a smile so big that it seemed to encompass his whole face. "Her name is Rebecca Anne Markham, and Darcy has been asking for you, Jesse, Zoey and Tanya after she sees her father, Liz and Sean for a few minutes."

The family went with Joshua while the rest stayed in the waiting room. Beth stood by the entrance, watching the door into Darcy's room.

"You would think she was a member of your family," Samuel said as he planted himself next to her.

"As we were growing up, I was like a big sister to her, Jesse and Zoey. So, yes, she does seem like a member of my family."

"That role came easily to you, didn't it?"

She tilted her head toward him, a question in her eyes. "As a big sister?"

"Yes."

"I guess so. That's really the only one I know except being a teacher."

"I bet your siblings think differently, especially Daniel. You were more a mother to him than a big sister."

She thought for a moment, her brow furrowed. "You're probably right. I am all he knows, since my mother died in childbirth. So my roles have been teacher, mother, sister."

"How about friend, leader, organizer—"

Beth laid her fingers against his lips. "Please, no more. I get the picture."

"Do you? You are invaluable to this town and the church. I don't think you realize that. You just go and do the things that need to be done and never really think anything about it. With your departure this summer you're trying to fill all your positions before you go. Most people don't do that. They walk away and don't look back."

Her cheeks tinged pink, Beth glanced toward Darcy's room. "Oh, I see the family leaving." She started forward, then stopped and turned back to him. "I appreciate what you said. Really I do. But if I hadn't done those jobs, someone else would have. That's the way Sweetwater is. We take care of what is ours, and that includes you and your family."

Samuel watched her enter Darcy's hospital room with the other members of her circle of friends. Her parting words washed over him and for a long moment he didn't feel so alone in the world.

Samuel entered the front door of the church and walked toward the sanctuary. He had begun to visit with God daily again, and he cherished this time before the day really started. Normally this was his day off, but he felt compelled to visit, to check and see if everything was all right. Inside, light streamed from the stained-glass windows to illuminate his path. He headed for the front pew and came to a halt halfway down the center aisle. He wasn't alone. Tanya sat on the front pew where he often did, with her head bowed, her body shaking with sobs. He hurried forward.

"Tanya, what's wrong?" He slid in beside her.

She lifted her tear-streaked face, a piece of paper crumpled in her hands. "Tom has asked me for a divorce. I…" Sobs racked her body again as she turned away.

Samuel drew her against him. "I'm so sorry, Tanya. Have you been able to see him lately, talk to him?"

She shook her head. "He refused to let me come after that time I went when he was injured. He was furious that I ignored his wishes then. What am I going to do?"

"Let me go visit Tom and talk with him."

Tanya latched on to Samuel's hands. "Please do. I know if he wants a divorce there is nothing I can really do to stop it. Please talk to him, make him understand I love him no matter what he did. He's Crystal's father. She needs him now more than ever."

As Samuel bowed his head to offer a prayer, he felt this was the right thing to do. He might not be able to talk Tom out of divorcing Tanya, but he had to try. Not only was Tanya hurting, but it was obvious Tom was, too.

"A picnic! What a lovely idea, Samuel," Beth said into the phone.

"Good. I'm glad you like it. Allie and Craig want to see some of the lake now that it is getting warmer. I'm counting on your preparing the food, since Aunt Mae is busy with Zoey and Jesse on the Fourth of July auction. You know how helpless I am in the kitchen."

"They're meeting without me?"

"Aunt Mae said something about you had great notes on each step of the planning and didn't want to bother you with the details, since you wouldn't be here for it."

"But still…" Beth couldn't voice aloud her dissatisfaction at not being asked to help, at least until she left Sweetwater. Yes, she had turned her duties over to others, but still she hadn't wanted to be totally out of the loop.

"Beth, you have to learn to turn it over to the ones doing it." Samuel lowered his voice. "Enjoy some of the free time with me and my family. It's the last week in March and spring break. You need to play some."

"Well, when you put it that way… Any orders on what you all want?" Beth stared out the picture window at the pear trees laden with white flowers and the red tulips and yellow daffodils gracing the length of Felicia's house across the street.

"I'll let you surprise us. I'll bring dessert and my two youngest children and pick you up in an hour."

"How about Jane?"

"That's the best piece of news I have. She's meeting some friends at the church to help clean up the garden. Joshua organized it."

"Maybe we should help them."

"Have you forgotten my black thumb? Besides, I think Jane wants me to stay away. Ryan is one of the group. He's been calling here the past week every night."

"Then I'll see you three in an hour."

When Beth hung up she sighed heavily, still bothered that she was left out of the planning for the auction. She'd done it for the past ten years. But with the letter she had received yesterday, she knew for certain she wouldn't be here come the Fourth of July. She would be in Brazil working at a mission along the Amazon River. She still couldn't believe how fast everything was proceeding. In the next few months she had a lot to do— getting her passport, getting a physical and a whole series of shots.

But for the moment she had a picnic to plan and an afternoon to spend with Samuel and his children. She noticed a bounce to her step as she walked into the kitchen. What was next—whistling while she worked? But she couldn't contain her excitement. For the trip or for seeing Samuel? She didn't know the answer and didn't care.

Opening the refrigerator, she inspected its contents, trying to decide what two young children would want to eat on a picnic. Remembering back to her picnics with her brothers and sister, she quickly settled on making peanut butter and jelly sandwiches with sliced fruit and chips. Nothing fancy, but then children rarely wanted that.

She set about preparing the food, then put on a new pair of jeans she had bought with Jesse the past weekend after their get-together at Alice's Café with Zoey, Tanya and Darcy, who had brought along her baby daughter. Wearing her new orange blouse and tennis shoes, Beth tied her curly hair back with an orange silk scarf, a few strands of hair escaping. She was ready to go when Samuel rang the doorbell exactly an hour after his phone call.

Beth grabbed a navy blue sweater in case she got cold from the breeze off the lake and went to answer the door. "Hi! I'm so glad you asked me to go with you all. I needed a reason not to do some yard work."

"I work hard to avoid yard work. Glad we think alike." Samuel pointed to a basket on the table in the foyer. "Is this the food?"

She nodded. "What's for dessert?"

"Nothing. The kids want to come back to the ice cream parlor on Main and have some after our picnic. Is that okay with you?"

"Ice cream. Let's see. Next to banana cream pie, vanilla ice cream with hot caramel topping is my favorite dessert, so I guess it's okay with me."

"I hear Miller Point is a nice place to have a picnic."

"There are several places around the lake that are nice. Miller Point is fine with me."

"With spring break the kids have been eager to do some things outside. Craig and Allie brought some fishing poles to see if they can catch anything. Do you fish?"

"Nope, but I don't mind watching."

Samuel lifted the basket and allowed Beth to go first. He shut the door and made sure it was locked before descending the steps. Beth slid into the front seat and turned to greet Allie and Craig.

"Will you help me pick some wildflowers? I've seen some pretty ones from the road," Allie said as her father started the car.

"Sure. There was a time I knew the names of a lot of them. But I haven't gone wild-flower picking in years." She'd been so busy doing other things she'd forgotten how much she liked doing something simple like that. She and her sister used to walk along the lake and collect wildflowers to put in a vase on the kitchen table. They had always tried to get as many different colors as possible. Her sister had called it a rainbow bouquet. "Miller Point is perfect for that. There's a meadow not far from the lake's edge."

Craig screwed up his face into a frown at the very mention of flowers. Beth added for his benefit, "You are welcome to help us, Craig. I don't want you to feel left out."

"No way. That's for girls."

"Son, when you get older, you'll realize giving flowers to a girl becomes very important to a guy," Samuel said with a smile.

"Not for me," Craig muttered, staring out the side window as his father drove toward Miller Point.

"What about Susie? Mary Ann says her older sister likes you and you like her," Allie said in a singsong voice.

"No, I don't!"

"Yes, you do. You talk to her when she calls." Allie stuck her tongue out at her brother, who returned the gesture.

Samuel slowed his car, pulled over and said, "If you two are going to fight, we can go home to do that."

Both crossed their arms, lifted their chins and turned to look out their respective car windows. Beth bit the inside of her cheek to keep a straight face. This little skirmish between brother and sister brought back bittersweet memories of raising her siblings. There had been times when they had been constantly at each other's throat and she had wondered if she would ever have any peace in the house again. Now she had more peace than she knew what to do with.

Samuel resumed driving. "Sorry about that, Beth."

"No problem. I'm used to it. You ought to hear some of the students at school."

Five minutes later Samuel pulled into a parking area near Miller Point. Allie and Craig were out of the car the second he turned off the engine. They raced toward the water, one going east along the sandy shore and the other west.

"I knew I was going to have a problem when I found out Allie's new best friend's older sister liked Craig. Allie is constantly teasing him and he isn't taking it very well."

"Sort of like he teases Jane about Ryan?"

"Yep. There are times I sneak out of the house and seek some quiet at the church."

Beth laughed. "I've been there. I know what you mean."

Samuel opened his door. "Let's spread the blanket under that maple over there." He gestured toward the largest tree in the area.

Carrying the blanket while Samuel took the basket, Beth walked beside him to the maple. Craig ran back to the car to get his fishing rod while Allie explored the shoreline, picking up some stones to examine and pocketing one.

After setting the blanket down and spreading it out so only part of it was shaded, Beth tossed back her head and let the warm rays of the sun bathe her face. Inhaling lungfuls of the rich air, she let the peacefulness of her surroundings seep into her. The chirping of the birds and the soothing serenade of the insects combined with the water lapping against the sandy beach to complete the ideal picture.

She turned toward Samuel, who had already opened the basket to peek inside. "Again I want to thank you for this wonderful suggestion. It's beautiful. Today no one should spend any time indoors."

"It's one of those perfect spring days that reconfirms God's presence." He closed the lid.

"Does the meal meet with your approval?"

"You could have brought just about anything and I wouldn't have cared less. I'm not a picky eater, as opposed to my daughters. One is a vegetarian and the other only likes peanut butter and jelly sandwiches, any kind of sweet and spaghetti." He snapped his fingers. "Oh, I almost forgot, and hamburgers and French fries."

"Not your healthiest food."

"Nope. I'm only hoping it's a brief stage she's moving through." He flipped his hand toward the basket. "But I can see you must have read Allie's mind. You have peanut butter and jelly sandwiches. How did you know?"

"Not many children their age hate PB and J sandwiches."

"True. You know children well."

"Raising three and teaching hundreds does have its advantages."

Allie raced toward the car and retrieved her fishing rod. She joined her brother, who sat on a large rock jutting out over the water. Passing her pole to Craig, Allie watched as he baited the line.

"What's he fishing with?"

"Bologna."

"Grant you, I'm not a fisherman—or is that

woman? Oh, well, I'm not one of those, but I've never heard of bologna being used to lure fish to your hook."

"Allie screams if we use anything live like worms." Samuel moved back to sit on the blanket. "Surprisingly they have caught some using bologna, so Craig goes along with it."

Beth eased down next to Samuel, everything about the day feeling so right. It seemed natural to her that they were sitting and watching the two children fish as though they had for years. Samuel was easy to talk to. He made her feel important, special, very much a woman. If she hadn't had her life planned, it would have been easy to fall for him. Why had someone come along when she had stopped looking for a husband, a man to love? She had to keep focused on her trip in the summer.

Samuel rested one arm on his bent knee, never taking his gaze off his children. "How are your plans coming along? Have you heard back from the organization?"

"Yes," she said with less excitement than she would have thought. "I received my acceptance a few days ago."

"Where are you going?"

"Brazil."

"Where the dart landed?"

"Yes, that was as good a way to decide as any. The world is full of places I haven't been to." Beth crossed her legs, stretched out in front of her. "I'm going to be assigned to a mission at the upper reaches of the Amazon just before the border with Peru."

"The Amazon! That's a far cry from Sweetwater."

"Yes, but what an adventure. I've decided to keep a journal of my travels. I may write a book one day. I've always wanted to, and this will be my chance to do good for God and fill pages and pages with the new things I've learned."

"I wish I could capture your enthusiasm and give some to Jane."

"Her grades are improving. She doesn't complain to me anymore while we're working."

"That's good, since you're doing her a favor. Have I thanked you in the past week?"

Beth smiled. "Yes, every time I come over."

"Okay, I've probably carried the appreciative-dad role just a little too far, but because of you Jane is doing better and she doesn't complain like she used to about going to school."

"Soon I'm going to approach her about using the resource room when she needs help. It's staffed with two special ed teachers who assist students on IEPs with their class work, any long-term assignments and taking tests in a quiet environment where there aren't very many distractions."

"She won't do it."

"She'll need something after I'm gone if she runs into any trouble. Right now she's using me, but next year I won't be here."

Samuel flexed his hands, then curled them into fists. "I know."

The tight edge to his voice caused Beth to angle her head to look him directly in the eyes. "I want her to learn to advocate for herself and not to be ashamed of needing help with certain projects. We all need help from time to time."

"From where I'm sitting you look pretty together."

"Well, I'm not all the time."

"When?"

"The night you took me to Andre's. I was a basket case."

He quirked a brow. "You were?"

"I haven't dated much. Not very good at it when I have. If you haven't noticed, I'm shy."

"You could have fooled me. Of course, I haven't dated much either."

"So neither one of us is an expert at dating."

"I know a solution to that."

"What?"

"Go out on another date with me."

Her heart skipped a beat, then began to pound. "I…" She was at a loss for words.

"If you don't say yes soon, I'm liable to be set back years with this dating."

"By all means, we wouldn't want that."

"Then it's a yes?"

"Yes," she said with a laugh.

Chapter Seven

Beth slipped from the extra-large booth at Alice's Café to grab the coffee. She poured some for Tanya and herself. "I'm glad Alice doesn't mind us monopolizing this table for several hours." She held up the glass pot. "Any other takers?"

"No, strictly tea for me." Zoey dunked her used tea bag into her hot water and added some sugar. "I'm thinking about getting another macadamia cookie. Anyone else want one?"

Darcy placed her hand over her stomach. "Not me. It's gonna be weeks, probably months, before I can fit into my clothes again. Dieting is the pits."

Jesse raised her mug. "Here's to the day when we don't have to watch our weight."

"I'm afraid I'd be dead by that time,"

Beth murmured, sitting again in the booth next to Tanya.

"Me, too." Tanya cupped her chin and rested her elbow on the table, looking despondent, deep lines carved into her expression.

"What's going on, Tanya?" Beth asked, realizing that for the past half hour her friend had said little.

A heavy sigh escaped Tanya's lips. "I didn't want to say anything, at least, not till the end, because I hate to put a damper on our gathering."

"Nonsense." Jesse waved her hand in the air. "That's what these gatherings are for. To help each other through the rough times. Has something else happened to Tom? Is he hurt again?"

Tanya shook her head, her eyes watering. "No, I..." She swallowed hard. "He wants a divorce. I received the papers a few days ago."

"You did! Why didn't you tell us immediately?" Zoey asked, stirring her green tea.

"I'm embarrassed." Tanya hung her head, staring into the black darkness of her coffee.

Beth laid her hand on her upper arm. "There's nothing for you to be embarrassed about. You can't control what Tom wants, especially with him in prison. Have you talked to him since you received the papers?"

"He doesn't want to talk with me or see me. I don't know what to do about it."

"Oh, Tanya, I'm so sorry." Tears pooled in Darcy's eyes and began to roll down her cheeks. "My hormones are running rampant." She wiped the wet tracks, only to have more tears flow. "I'm not gonna be much help. You talk to her, Beth. You're always so sensible."

Beth slipped her arm about Tanya's shoulders and pulled her friend toward her. "Give it some time. Maybe he'll come to his senses."

"I don't think so, but Reverend Morgan is going up there today to talk to Tom. He came by this morning to see how I was. I don't know what I would have done if it wasn't for our new reverend. His words have kept me focused on what's important—my daughter. I can't let this cause a setback for me. I just can't."

"Samuel does have a way about him," Beth murmured, picturing the man under discussion.

"*Samuel* does?" Jesse arched a brow. "Hmm. That sounds awfully cozy, if you ask me."

Beth shot Jesse an exasperated look. "I'm not asking you. Don't you start, Jesse Blackburn."

Tanya smiled. "You two need to stop it before Alice throws us out for causing a scene. Beth, don't you know you'll never be able to change Jesse's nature? She's a born matchmaker."

"I would refer to her as a born busybody."

"Busybody!" Jesse clasped her chest, her mouth forming a large *O*. "I can't believe you said that about me."

"If I don't shut you down immediately, you'll weave a fantasy with me marrying our minister and having his baby."

The grin on Jesse's face was pure mischief. "I don't have to. You're doing a great job of it yourself."

"Now I know why Beth is sitting at one end of the table and you at the other." Zoey shook her head, then took a swallow of her drink. "If I remember correctly, we were going to discuss Crystal's birthday coming up in a few weeks. She'll be fourteen—only two years to her sweet sixteen birthday."

"My daughter is growing up," Tanya said,

pulling herself together as the conversation turned to Crystal's birthday.

Beth relaxed back, noticing that Tanya was no longer teary eyed. In fact, she was sipping her coffee and throwing herself into the party planning for her daughter. While listening to the discussion, Beth said a silent prayer that Samuel's trip to the prison would be successful.

Samuel sat at the bare table in the bare room at the prison, waiting for Tom Bolton's appearance—if he appeared, and Samuel was beginning to feel he wouldn't. He checked his watch for the third time and wondered what he should do if the man refused to see him, too. As the minutes ticked away, frustration coiled in Samuel's stomach until it ached.

Then suddenly the door swung open and a man walked in with a guard behind him. Tom limped to the table, his eyes downcast. But even though his face was averted, Samuel saw the swollen lip and cut under his eye. He blew out a breath of air, hoping God would guide him in what he should say to this man.

After Tom eased into the chair and the guard backed away to stand by the door,

Tanya's husband finally lifted his gaze to Samuel's. The despair in his eyes shook Samuel to the core of his being. This was a man without hope.

Tom blinked, and the despair was replaced with anger. With his arms folded over his chest, his hands fisted and his eyes narrowed, Tom said nothing as he stared at Samuel.

Samuel coated his dry throat and scooted his chair closer to the table, placing his elbows on its wooden surface. "Your wife asked me to come and see how you were."

A nerve in the man's jaw twitched. "How does it look to you?"

"You're not doing too well."

"I guess we can't say you're blind, Reverend."

"What happened?" Samuel indicated the cuts on Tom's face.

"I walked into a brick wall. An occupational hazard in here."

"Have you reported—" Samuel glanced at the guard "—the brick wall?"

Tom shrugged, all expression shutting down completely.

"Is there anything you want me to do? Maybe I can talk to someone for you."

Again another shrug.

"I will pray for you."

"Suit yourself. It won't help, reverend. Nothing does."

The man's words held no hope, and the expression in his eyes was weary as though he didn't care anymore about anything.

"Perhaps we can pray now."

"I stopped praying the day Crystal fell from the horse. What good is praying to a God who allows your baby to be hurt?"

Hearing Tom's anger, which mirrored his own at one time, made Samuel wince. Was that how he had sounded after Ruth died? He was ashamed of those feelings now. No good came of them except to throw his family, his life, into chaos. He wanted to help Tom see that.

"You have a beautiful daughter who is full of life. She isn't letting the fact she's in a wheelchair slow her down. She's—"

"Stop right there, Reverend, or this meeting is over. I won't listen to you talk about God and His grand plan that somehow involves my daughter being crippled. So if that's all you came to talk about, then I guess you wasted your time."

"No, that's not all," Samuel murmured, staring at Tom's closed expression. The silence lengthened into a long moment while Samuel tried to decide how to approach Tom about the divorce. He couldn't think of any way but straightforward. "Tanya doesn't want a divorce."

Tom blinked rapidly several times, then that blank look reappeared. "That's too bad, because I do."

"Will you at least see her and talk to her about it?"

Tanya's husband shook his head. "No use in wasting either one's time."

"She doesn't feel it's a waste."

"Too bad." Tom scraped the chair back and rose. "You've wasted enough of my valuable time. I have to get back to work."

The almost monotone quality to his voice sent chills down Samuel's spine. Desperation made him ask, "Don't you want to know how your family is doing?"

Tom closed his eyes for a few seconds, then opened them and looked right at Samuel, no expression whatsoever on his face. "They're better off without me. Now, if you'll excuse me."

Tom was at the door when Samuel said, "Your daughter misses you."

The man's back stiffened, but he didn't

turn around or say anything to Samuel's last remark. When the guard and Tom left, Samuel scanned the bleak decor. It mirrored his feelings. He made his way out of the room and toward the guard at the end of the hall. The only result of this meeting with Tom was that he needed to prepare Tanya for the worst.

Lord, help me to be there for her in her time of need. Guide me in what I need to say to help her through this. And please be with Tom. He has lost all hope and needs it—and You—more than anyone.

Beth paused on the stone path, hesitant to go any farther into the Garden of Serenity. Samuel sat on a wooden bench near the pond with his head bent, his hands clasped together and his elbows resting on his thighs. He was a man lost in prayer.

She'd started to leave when he raised his head and peered at her. No, he was simply a man lost. His dejected expression ripped through her composure and sent her forward, her only thought to comfort. "What's wrong?"

The haunted look in his eyes shifted as though he was trying to mask it but was not quite able to. "I went to see Tom in prison."

Beth settled next to him on the bench. "I

know. Tanya mentioned it earlier today at Alice's Café."

"Yeah. I forgot about your meeting with the others." He scanned the area as if he finally realized they were sitting in the middle of the church garden. "How did you find me?"

"Jane said you headed over to the church when you returned from your trip. I saw you as I was heading into the building to find you." With only a few inches separating them, she felt tension emanating from him and her concern grew. "What happened with Tom? Will he see Tanya?"

"No. He is adamant about that—and the divorce." Samuel took hold of her hand and gripped it. "I couldn't help him, Beth. I tried, but he wouldn't listen. He has turned away from the Lord."

Even though Samuel's clasp was tight, what unnerved her about his touch was its intensity, its desperation. "Sometimes there's nothing we can do to make a person listen to reason. You can't make a person believe in God's purpose."

"I have no business being a minister. I can't help my parishioners. I can't help my family. I can't help myself."

Beth sucked in a deep breath and held it until her lungs felt on fire. Such despair wrenched her heart, constricting it into a painful lump that seemed to barely beat in her chest. She covered their clasped hands with her other one and angled her body so she faced him. "Where in the world has that idea come from?"

His darkened gaze shifted to hers. "Take a good look around you."

Her throat closed around the words she wanted to say. She swallowed several times before she felt she could talk above the barest whisper. "I have. Today I sat with Tanya and listened to her sing your praises for the help you have given her through this difficult time. That doesn't sound like a person who hasn't been able to help someone. You can't help everyone. I've learned that the hard way as a teacher. You try your best and hope you can, but it doesn't always work."

"When I came to Sweetwater, I felt this was my last chance to prove myself as a minister."

She hadn't thought it possible, but his eyes became even darker, as though turmoil churned in their depths. "Last chance? You had a good record as a minister."

"Not since my wife's death. I guess you could call what has happened to me a crisis of faith. So how can a minister who is questioning God's purpose in his own life help others see God's purpose?"

"When my mother died, I was angry at God for taking her away and leaving me with three siblings to raise. I didn't know how I was going to make it. Raise them. Finish college. Have a life. We all have times in our lives when we wonder about the plans God has for us, even reject the direction He wants us to go. Just because you are a minister doesn't mean you're immune to doubts or questions concerning your faith."

"But Tom still won't see Tanya. He's still proceeding with the divorce."

"And we'll be there for Tanya. We can't control Tom's actions, but we can help Tanya deal with them."

He released a deep breath through pursed lips.

"You must keep talking to God. He's there. He's listening. Always," she added.

"I'm trying."

"That's all you can do. Try your best. As far as your family goes, your children adore you. Yes, Jane is rebelling, but that's typical of a teenager. I've seen some growth over the past few months, mainly because she knows you'll love her no matter what. That's powerful stuff when you're dealing with raging hormones."

Samuel smiled, one corner of his mouth lifting. "I guess you should know, since you've raised three teenagers and dealt with hundreds on a daily basis."

"Yes, the teacher knows best."

He chuckled. "I thought that was the father knows best."

"As my students say, *whatever*."

Samuel straightened, removing his hand from hers. "Did you need me for something?"

For a few seconds Beth battled disappointment that they were not holding hands any longer. Then she thought of the danger in that and pushed her conflicting feelings to the back of her mind. "We were planning Crystal's birthday party in a few weeks and wanted it to be a surprise for her. Do you think we could use the rec hall for the party? Her birthday is on a Wednesday and she has youth choir practice that evening."

"That's a wonderful idea. We can have the party after the practice."

"That was what I was hoping you would say."

"What can I do to help?"

"Nothing. Tanya, Jesse, Darcy, Zoey and I have it all planned. We'll just need your presence."

"You've got that." Samuel rose and offered his hand to help her to her feet. When she stood, he moved back a step and said, "Now, about that date we discussed going on. How about going to the movies? Maybe next Saturday night?"

Date. There was that word again. "That sounds fine." *That sounds dangerous,* an inner voice taunted. "Why don't you come over for dinner at my house beforehand?"

"We can go out. I don't want you to go to any trouble."

"I know we could go out, but I like to cook and I would like to cook for you." What in the world had she just admitted to him? The ground she was standing on seemed to tremble.

His smile this time was full-fledged. "Then I can't say no. What time?"

"Let's say seven. We can go to the later movie."

"You've got yourself a date."

That was what she was afraid of, she thought, staring at his heart-melting look, the dimple in his left cheek. If she stayed any longer, she would end up a pool of liquid at his feet. She backed away.

"I'd better go. Even though I'm officially on spring break, I have tons of papers to grade. The exciting life of an English teacher." She heard herself rambling and winced inwardly.

She spun about to leave.

"Beth."

His voice called back to her. She glanced over her shoulder, steeling herself.

"Thanks for everything."

Her resolve not to fall for him was fast crumbling about her. "You're welcome. You would do the same for me." She hurried away before she decided to stay… Something she *knew* was dangerous.

"Would you like to come inside for a cup of decaf coffee?" Beth asked as Samuel escorted her to her front porch Saturday night after the movie.

He took her key from her and inserted it into her lock, then opened the door. "That sounds like a nice way to end this evening.

Besides, I want to help you clean up the dishes from the dinner."

"You don't have to do that."

"I know. But I want to."

"You're a keeper. A man who wants to do dishes."

"And I do windows, too."

"How about bathrooms? That's the room I hate to clean the most." Inside her house Beth shut the front door and slipped out of her heavy sweater, draping it over a chair in the foyer.

"I can't say I'm too fond of doing the bathroom either, especially after the children use it. Thankfully Aunt Mae takes care of the housework. She has managed to get my children to help, which was something I wasn't very successful at."

"I have to admit I found it easier to do the work than plead with and prod my brothers and sister into doing their chores." She walked through the living room and dining room into the kitchen, heading for the coffeemaker. "Have a seat. This shouldn't take long."

"What about those dishes?"

"They can wait a little while longer."

"You won't get an argument out of me. What did you think of the movie?"

Beth filled the glass carafe with water and poured it into the coffee machine, then switched it on. "I liked it. It was light and funny. I wasn't in the mood for anything heavy this evening. It's nice to see two older people falling in love. So many movies are about young people, as though anyone over forty doesn't have a love life."

"I think Jane feels that way about anyone over thirty. By the way, speaking of my oldest daughter, thank you."

"What for?"

"We got her report card right after spring break and she passed all her subjects. I don't think that would have happened if you hadn't intervened."

Beth sat across from Samuel at her kitchen table. "This next nine weeks will be even better. I haven't quite convinced her to use the resource room, but I'm making headway. Hopefully by the end of the semester she will use it for the end-of-semester tests. I think it will help her to take them in a quiet environment with few distractions."

He leaned forward, clasping her hand. "What am I going to do without you next year? What's Jane going to do?"

Beth's heart thudded in her chest, its beating thundering against her eardrums. "You two will be fine." A sadness at the thought of leaving her hometown encased Beth in an icy shroud. She shivered.

"Cold?"

"No—yes. Truthfully, I am a little afraid of striking out on my own. I've never been very adventurous and I certainly haven't had a chance to travel much. I've only been to a few places, the farthest being Chicago, which isn't that far. I haven't been able to learn much of the language. What if I can't and no one understands me?"

He squeezed her hand, a gleam twinkling in his eyes. "You'll do just fine. Gesturing and body language can go a long way until you get the hang of Portuguese. I have confidence in you. You can do anything you set your mind to."

The scent of coffee brewing saturated the kitchen, adding an extra warmth to the atmosphere between them. Beth relaxed against the back of the chair, listening for the dripping to stop. "You sure know how to make a woman feel special."

"That's easy. You are special."

In that moment she felt very feminine and even pretty with Samuel's gaze trained on her, his total attention focused on her as though she was the only woman alive for him. How could a woman not feel special under those circumstances? How was she going to walk away from such a wonderful man, who made her experience things she never had?

The coffee finished perking, and Beth rose to withdraw two mugs from the cabinet above the machine. After pouring the dark brew into the cups, she asked, "Milk? Sugar?"

"Three heaping spoonfuls of sugar, please."

Surprise widened her eyes. "I can just give you the bowl of sugar and you can have it straight."

"In the army some of the coffee I had to drink was so bad that I'm not sure it was really coffee. I had to do something to make it drinkable. Now I can't have coffee without lots of sugar."

"I have my coffee blended for me. It's a shame you have to mask its rich flavor with sugar."

"Okay. Two spoonfuls. I can compromise when I have to."

Beth added the sugar to his mug, then

brought it over to the table and set it in front of him. She sat catercorner to him and took a tentative sip of her coffee. She loved this blend with a hint of vanilla in it.

Samuel curled his fingers around the handle and drank his doctored brew. "Mmm. This is good. We could have used you in the army."

"Maybe before I leave I can wean you off so much sugar in your coffee."

A cloud descended over his expression. "Anything is possible. How's Crystal's birthday party coming along?"

"Great. Everything's in place. Planning this has really helped Tanya take her mind off the divorce. That and your help."

"My help?"

"Don't play innocent with me. Tanya's told me about the couple of times you've stopped by her house to check up on her and talk to her. Your counseling means a lot to her. She's gone through a great deal in the past few years."

"She's lucky to have friends like you."

"I've seen Craig paying a lot of attention to Crystal during Sunday-school class lately. I think he likes her."

"He called someone last night and had a fit

when Allie tried to listen. I got the feeling he was talking to a girl. Maybe it was Crystal or Susie."

"It's spring. Love is in the air."

"Is that it?" Merriment flashed in his gaze as it locked with hers. "She's an older woman. Do you think that could work?"

"Possibly," Beth answered, thinking of the few years' age difference between her and Samuel.

Silence stretched between them—visually connected but separated by a table. His look dropped to her mouth and her lips tingled. Cradling the mug between her hands, she sipped her coffee, her gaze on Samuel the whole time.

He reached across the table and took her mug, putting it down. Then he feathered his finger along her jawline before tracing the outline of her mouth. She inhaled a sharp breath. The roughened texture of his fingertip sent chills down her body.

"I don't know how you ever thought of yourself as plain. You aren't plain at all."

His words washed over her, making her care even more for this man sitting in her kitchen as though he belonged there. "With you I never have."

"Good." His hand delved into the curls of her hair and cupped the back of her head.

Tension coiled in her stomach. She was falling in love with a man who still loved his deceased wife, who wasn't over her death.

Samuel rose and drew her to her feet, his hand still in her hair. He moved so close she was sure he could feel and hear her heart pounding. His scent surrounded her as though wrapping her in a protective cocoon. He tilted her head and angled his, slanting his lips over hers.

His kiss rocked her to her core. She felt as if she were floating in the air, her heart soaring. It wouldn't take much to want to center her whole life around this man.

Panic began to eat at her composure. How could she fall in love now of all times? Samuel Morgan, and especially his family of three children, did not fit into her plans for the future—plans she'd had for years.

Chapter Eight

Beth stiffened in his arms. Samuel pulled away, dazed by the reaction that had taken hold of him when his mouth had covered hers. He felt as though he had come home. That wasn't possible. Quickly he stepped back, dropping his arms to his sides. Guilt began to gnaw at his insides. How could he forget Ruth so easily? He shouldn't have kissed Beth. They were only friends.

From the expression in her eyes, he realized her conflicting emotions raged inside as his did. She touched her mouth, rubbing her fingertips across her lips as he had done only a moment before. As he wanted to do again. He took another step back, shocked at the direction his thoughts were taking him—away from Ruth, his high school sweetheart.

He could not place his heart in jeopardy again. Beth was leaving in a few months—she had made that very clear from the beginning. He still loved his wife, even if she was gone. He couldn't betray those feelings so easily. Easily? He laughed silently at that thought. There was nothing easy about the war waging inside him. Beth made him feel like a man again. She made him feel whole, as though the fragmented parts that had split with Ruth's death were coming together.

He wouldn't apologize for the kiss, but he did say, "I shouldn't have done that. I—I'd better go."

She didn't stop him when he turned to leave. Her gaze pierced him as he headed toward the door. Outside on her porch the cool spring air flowed over him, carrying on its breeze the scent of newly blooming hyacinths from the bed in front of her house.

Why had he kissed her?

He didn't want to ruin their friendship. What if he had? He thought of their talks over the past few months and didn't know what he would do if she avoided him because of the kiss.

But too quickly summer would be here and she would be gone. Maybe it was for the best they kept their distance. As he walked toward his car he turned to the Lord, as he was doing more and more of late for guidance.

"Are you mad at Samuel?" Zoey asked while standing back and watching the children pour into the rec hall right after choir practice Wednesday evening.

Beth glanced at her friend. "Mad? What gave you that idea?"

"Usually you two are talking constantly with each other. Tonight you haven't exchanged one word and only one look that I could tell. Something's going on."

Beth stepped away from the children gathering to surprise Crystal. Tanya was going to wheel her daughter into the room on the pretext she had forgotten something at the piano. Beth leaned toward Zoey and whispered, "He kissed me the other night."

"That's great!"

"Shh." Beth glanced about, making sure no one heard Zoey's remark. Thankfully everyone's attention, even Darcy's and Jesse's was on the door into the rec hall. "No, it isn't a good thing. I'm leaving in a few months. Everything's settled except getting my passport in the mail, getting my physical and shots and packing."

"Beth, it's okay to do something spontaneous. You always have your life planned down to the last detail. Falling in love doesn't work that way."

"He kissed me. That's all. Who said anything about falling in love?" Beth could hear the panic in her voice and knew by the arched eyebrow that Zoey had, too. Again Beth looked around, hoping no one was listening. She was having a tough time explaining this to Zoey, let alone anyone else.

The children searched for hiding places while Jesse turned off the lights and told everyone to be quiet.

Zoey sidled closer to Beth and brought her hand up to shield her lips while she whispered, "I've seen you two together. You're perfect. That's why when you didn't speak to him on Sunday after the church service as you usually do, I knew something was up. You two actually avoided each other. Then tonight the same thing happened."

"Shh. You don't want to spoil the surprise for Crystal."

"I'm not through discussing this, Beth Coleman."

"Yeah. That's what I'm afraid of."

Tanya opened the door to the rec hall and wheeled Crystal in. Someone snickered.

"Gee, Crystal, it's sure dark in here. I'd better turn on the light or I'm bound to run you into something." Tanya flipped the switch.

The children jumped up from behind chairs and the couch and yelled, "Surprise!"

Crystal's features lit with a big grin. She moved herself into the center of the room, scanning the group converging on her.

Craig playfully slugged Sean. "You almost blew the surprise."

Sean's face turned beet-red. "I couldn't help it. Cindy bet me I couldn't keep quiet."

"And you didn't. You lose." Cindy stepped around Sean and handed Crystal her present.

All the other kids began stacking gifts onto Crystal's lap until she giggled and said, "Uncle! No more. I can't see over the presents." One slid off her lap and thudded to the tile floor.

Jesse ran over to the fourteen-year-old, picked up the dropped gift and relieved her of some of the other wrapped boxes.

Beth watched the exchange, so glad the party was a success. She noticed tears gathering in Tanya's eyes as she looked on the scene. A lump lodged in Beth's throat, and she turned away before she, too, started to cry. Her gaze found Samuel in the doorway with Allie in front of him, his hand on her shoulder. Allie held a present, but hadn't made a move toward Crystal yet. Samuel said something to Allie, then looked directly at Beth.

Across the room she felt the connection as though it were a physical link that bound them. She experienced their kiss all over again, an awareness shivering down her spine, her pulse racing, her lips tingling. All this from a mere look!

She was in deeper than she had originally thought. He affected her on so many different levels—all dangerous to her carefully made plans and dreams of the future.

"Are you going to stand there and ignore our minister all night?" Zoey whispered, giving her a gentle shove toward him.

"I have a job to do. I have to dish up the ice cream in a few minutes and you have to cut the cake to serve with the ice cream."

"Oh, yeah. Thanks for reminding me." Zoey scurried across the room toward Samuel.

Beth shook her head. Sometimes her

friends could be so annoying. Usually it was Jesse who tried to fix people up, not Zoey. Well, she would be gone soon and then she wouldn't have to worry about that. But for some reason the thought of traveling and seeing some of the world didn't perk her up as it should have.

While Crystal opened her presents Beth made her way toward the kitchen to get the ice cream from the freezer. She heard the child's laughter and it filled her heart with joy. She would miss the chance to teach Crystal in a few years. For that matter, she wouldn't be instructing *any* of her friends' children. She hadn't really thought about that until now.

In the kitchen Beth paused, thinking that her mind was in turmoil too much lately. Change was good—she needed change. Her life had become so predictable and dull. She could serve the Lord and see the world. Great solution. Great plan.

With her resolve firmed, she walked to the counter. Rummaging in the drawer, she found the ice cream scoop and withdrew it.

She started to shut the drawer when she heard Samuel say, "Hold it. I need the cake slicer."

Zoey! She should have figured her friend

was up to something when she hurried over to Samuel. Beth rolled her eyes toward the ceiling, then grabbed the utensil for him, berating Zoey the whole time. She was definitely getting as bad as Jesse. If she was going to be around long enough, she would love to give Zoey a taste of her own medicine. She could think of a few men she could fix Zoey up with.

With the cake slicer in hand, Beth spun about to give it to Samuel and almost stabbed him in the chest because of his proximity. She jerked back, murmuring, "I'm sorry." The utensil clanged to the kitchen counter next to Beth. "I didn't know you were there."

He grinned. "I thought you heard me approach. I meant to reach around you and get the cake slicer."

She'd been so lost in thought about what Zoey had done that she hadn't heard a thing. Her friends were making her crazy. No, that wasn't quite right. Her seesawing emotions concerning Samuel were making her crazy. She needed to get a handle on things. Their relationship needed to get back to the way it was last month or even last week before "the kiss."

"Thankfully no harm was done." Her

breathing shallow, Beth pushed the drawer closed and placed several feet between them.

He stared at her, his gaze roaming over her features in a leisurely examination that only made her more self-conscious. The silence in the kitchen, which lengthened uncomfortably, was broken only by an occasional loud laugh from the rec hall.

Not taking her gaze from him, she shifted from one foot to the other, her mouth so parched she was afraid a gallon of water wouldn't satisfy her. "Are you slicing the cake?" She asked the first thing that popped into her mind. *Duh, Beth, of course he was, or why else would he be getting the cake slicer?*

"Yes. Zoey said something about retrieving some items from her car for the party."

Yeah, she just bet her friend had "some items" in her car. She would be curious to see what Zoey managed to scrounge up. "Then I guess we'd better get out there before the natives get restless."

Crystal finished opening her last present as Beth and Samuel emerged from the kitchen. Jesse, Darcy and Tanya all smiled toward Beth as though they knew a secret no one else did.

"It's time for cake and ice cream," Tanya announced.

"Let's sing happy birthday to Crystal first." Jesse waved the group of children toward the table where the cake was.

After everyone gathered around with Crystal in the center, the kids launched into the song, yelling and clapping at the end. The huge grin hadn't left Crystal's face the whole time.

"I think that's our cue to cut and scoop." Beth put some chocolate ice cream on the plate next to the first piece of chocolate cake with white frosting, then handed it to Crystal.

For the next ten minutes Beth scooped ice cream while Samuel stood next to her only a few inches away and sliced pieces of cake for all the children and grown-ups. The rec hall grew quiet as everyone found a place to sit and eat their treat.

"There are two pieces left. Do you want the one with a lot of frosting or the other one?" Samuel slid the cake with extra frosting, because it was a corner piece, onto one of the pink princess paper plates.

"I should say the one without much frosting, but I won't. I love the frosting the most."

Beth lifted the scoop filled with ice cream. "Want any?"

He nodded. "I can't pass up chocolate."

After she gave him what he had requested, she looked about for a chair to sit in. The only place available was the bench in the alcove or the floor. She headed for the alcove at the same time Samuel did. He glanced at her, then at the bench and shrugged.

After he eased onto the bench next to Beth, he said, "You know we need to talk about it."

"'It' meaning…?" She knew very well what he was referring to, but she wasn't going to be the one to say the word.

"The kiss. I'm not sorry I kissed you."

When she allowed herself to think about it, she wasn't either. But the kiss did complicate their relationship, which she was desperately trying to keep as simple as possible. "I'm not either, but where do we go from here?"

"I guess it's hard to go back to the way things were before I kissed you."

"Yes."

"To tell you the truth, Beth, I don't know the answer to that question. Maybe you should forget the kiss."

Forget the kiss? That could possibly be one of the hardest things she'd had to do in a long time. But because he was acting so casual about the kiss, Beth said, "Sure. We're friends, and friends kiss each other from time to time." *Yeah, right, Beth. If you keep saying that, you might convince yourself of the truth in that statement when the sun burns out.*

Samuel murmured something that sounded like a yes. He stuffed the last bite of cake into his mouth and rose. "I need to see how the adult choir practice is coming along. Bye."

He hurried away so quickly he didn't hear her say goodbye. It was just as well. If they had talked any more about kissing, she was afraid sweat would have beaded her brow and rolled down her face. How would she have explained that, when the hall was cool?

Samuel escaped from the rec hall before he did something crazy like kiss Beth in front of his parishioners. How did he think he could calmly talk about the kiss and not want to do it again? Especially since the past few days that kiss had dominated his thoughts.

She was leaving soon. He couldn't risk getting hurt—not again. He was just beginning to piece his life back together—partially due to the presence of Beth in his life as well as his family's. He had recited those same reasons not to get involved with Beth so many times over the past few days he wanted to pound something in frustration.

With a groan Samuel leaned back against the hall's wooden doors. He was in big trouble. He was afraid his heart was already involved with Beth to the point that he was going to be hurt when she left Sweetwater. Staying away from her was probably the best plan for him. He walked toward the sanctuary. He needed to feel close to God. He needed His help.

"What do you mean you haven't seen Samuel in several weeks except at church?"

Beth lifted the cup of coffee to her lips and took a drink. "Exactly that, Jesse. He's never around when I go to tutor Jane and the couple of times I've been at the church other than Sunday he hasn't been there, or at least I haven't seen him there."

Jesse shifted in the booth at Alice's Café, glancing out the picture window at the main street of Sweetwater. "It sounds like he's avoiding you."

"You think?"

Her friend frowned. "And you said it began after he kissed you and then tried to talk to you about that kiss?"

"Correct." Beth folded her arms and placed them on the table between her and Jesse.

"It's obvious. He's got cold feet."

"I know that. Jesse, I might not date a lot, but I do know what's going on here. And truthfully, Samuel's doing the right thing. Our relationship was heading toward more than friendship, and that isn't a good thing."

"Why not?"

"Because I'm committed to leaving in seven weeks and Samuel is committed to the memory of his deceased wife."

"Are you so sure about that? He kissed you!"

"One simple little kiss." She wasn't about to tell Jesse that to her it hadn't been a simple *or* little kiss. After all, her friend was the town matchmaker. Beth caught sight of Zoey and Tanya opening the door to the café and added, "Not another word, please. I only told you about the kiss so you'd quit bugging me about Samuel."

"Fine. My lips are sealed." Jesse made a motion of turning a key by her mouth. "Even

though I think we could all put our heads together and come up with a plan for you."

Beth growled her frustration as Darcy
called out to Zoey and Tanya to hold the door.
Darcy wheeled in a stroller with Rebecca in
it, sound asleep, looking the spitting image
of Joshua.

When the three ladies began settling into
the oversize booth, Beth said, "I won't be
able to stay too long. I'm tutoring Jane this
afternoon. She has a research project due
next week and we've been working extra to
get it in. Let me sit on the outside." She slid
across and stood while the others situated
themselves.

Darcy winked. "Are you sure that's the
only reason you spend so much time over at
the reverend's house? I've gone by several
times and have seen your car parked in the
driveway."

"I don't see Samuel. He's been very busy
lately. I'm seeing Jane," Beth said through
clenched teeth.

Tanya took the menu lying on the table
and flipped it open. "Yeah, he keeps going to
the prison to try and get Tom to meet with
him. Tom's refusing ever since that first
meeting last month."

"Tanya, I'm so sorry. I know how much you were hoping that Tom would listen to reason." Darcy moved the blanket, revealing Rebecca in a cute pink dress with bunnies on it.

"The divorce is going through and there isn't anything to be done. Tom's turned away from God. That breaks my heart."

"Maybe when he's not so angry he'll find the Lord again." Beth checked her watch and rose. "I'd better get a move on. Sorry to cut this short, but some of you were late."

"With three kids it's hard to be on time for anything," Zoey said with a laugh. "And I brought Tanya, so that was why she was late."

Darcy gestured toward Rebecca. "She's my reason."

"That's okay. Beth and I discussed the men in our lives."

"Jesse, there are no men in my life unless you count my two brothers."

"Oh, yes, I'd forgotten. You haven't been dating anyone."

The twinkle in Jesse's eyes almost made Beth stay. She was afraid the second she left she and Samuel would be the subject of conversation at the table. "I've gone out a few times with Samuel. That's all. No big deal." She turned quickly away from her friends and headed for the door. She didn't want to dig a hole any deeper by staying and debating that with them.

Ten minutes later she arrived at Samuel's house and Jane greeted her at the door with a huge smile on her face.

"I don't have much left to do. I worked this morning. Ryan has asked me to go to the movies with him and some of his friends. Dad said yes so long as I was in a group."

Beth entered the house. "Your dad is here?" The second the question was out of her mouth she bit the inside of her cheek to keep from saying anything else.

"Yes, he's in his office writing the sermon for tomorrow."

Beth wanted to ask, "And he knew I was coming?" but refrained from making her interest too obvious. And she was definitely interested in Samuel, no matter what she had told herself or him earlier. Just the mention of his name sent her heart thudding against her chest.

Jane walked toward the dining room, where she had set up her work and the laptop she was composing on.

For the next hour Beth helped Jane hone the final draft of her research paper for history. Every sound coming from the direction of the office caused Beth to tense as though Samuel would walk into the room any second and change her whole world. By the time Jane printed out her final copy of the paper, Beth had drunk two tall glasses of water to moisten her parched throat and mouth.

Her nerves stretched taut, she read over the four pages Jane had written. "You've done a good job with this. Your history teacher will be proud of your hard work."

Jane beamed as she gathered up her papers and closed the laptop.

Footsteps from the hallway pushed Beth's composure to the edge. She slid a glance toward the door and stopped breathing for a few seconds. Samuel propped one shoulder against the jamb and smiled at her. Casual. Laid back. Appealing. Charming. All those words floated through her mind as she stared at him—blatantly, as if no one else was in the room.

Jane cleared her throat. "I'm going to go get ready for the movies."

She heard the teenager's words as though coming from afar. Every sense attuned to

Samuel, Beth rose, their gazes linked. She wet her lips, then swallowed several times but nothing relieved the dryness that held her.

"I've missed you."

Samuel's words eroded her composure completely. She melted against the chair, gripping its back to keep from falling. No words came to mind.

"I've missed our talks."

That statement sparked her anger like flint against a stone. "I've been here every Monday, Tuesday and Thursday afternoon. Where have you been?" There was a part of her that was amazed she had said anything to him about his avoidance of her while she was tutoring Jane. But the other part cheered her on. She knew it was for the best that they not carry their friendship to the next level, but it was so nice to feel like a real woman for once.

"Usually at my office in the church until I see you leave."

His words caused her to blink in surprise. She didn't know what to say to the truth.

He chuckled, raising his hand, palm outward. "I admit it. I don't know what to do about us."

"Us?" she squeaked out, her voice breathless.

"Yes, us. There is an us, Beth, and you can't deny that."

"I'm not. But we won't go anywhere."

"How about we just enjoy the time we have together? I need practice dating. You need practice dating."

"We're going to practice dating?"

He nodded. "That's what I propose."

The word *propose* sent a whole different image into her mind than what he had intended. She saw herself in a long white gown, standing before a minister who wasn't Samuel because he was next to her, holding her hand. "I guess that wouldn't hurt us. I've had fun on our two dates."

"Then let's make it a third one. Jesse has invited me to a dinner at her house."

"She has?" Beth clenched the wooden slat on the back of the chair, determined to leave soon and have a word with her friend.

"Yes, she said something about inviting you and I told her I would, since I knew you would be here today."

"Do you know what one of Jesse's little dinner parties means?"

His eyes twinkled. "Yes, I've heard rumors. That's why I thought I would make it easy on her and invite you myself."

"You're too kind. I would have made her sweat some."

"I thought about doing that, but she does a lot for the church."

"You know the whole evening we'll be subjected to her matchmaking schemes."

"I think we can weather them—together."

Together. The one word stuck in her mind and kept her from thinking of anything beyond that. Again that image of her in the long white gown popped into her mind.

Worry creased his face. "Beth?"

She pulled herself away from her riotous thoughts and said, "You don't know Jesse when she sets her mind on something."

"She doesn't know me."

Some of the tension siphoned from Beth as she took in Samuel's smile, his relaxed stance. "True. We shouldn't make this easy for her."

"What do you have in mind?"

A plan began to formulate in her thoughts. She circled the table and came to stand in front of Samuel. "Let me tell you what we should do."

Chapter Nine

"You two seem awfully chummy tonight," Jesse said, handing Beth a platter with the steaks on it.

"We thought we would make it easier for you."

Jesse narrowed her gaze on Beth. "You're up to something. I can feel it."

Beth touched her chest. "Who, me?"

"Yeah, you." Jesse held the door open to allow Beth to exit the house first. "Last week you were avoiding him and now I can hardly keep you two apart."

"We've given up fighting our feelings."

Jesse's eyes grew round, and she hung back by the door, her voice low as she bent toward her to ask, "You aren't leaving this summer, then?"

"I didn't say that. Can't a gal date without it having to lead to anything permanent? I want to enjoy my last few months here. I enjoy being with Samuel." Even though she and Samuel had planned to play up their attraction, Beth was discovering she wasn't really playacting at all. She meant every word she'd said to Jesse.

Her friend's eyes widened even more. "This doesn't sound like you." She stepped back. "Come to think of it, you aren't dressed like the Beth I've known for years. What have you done with her?"

Beth laughed. "I've come to my senses. You, Darcy, Zoey and Tanya have been pushing me to wear brighter clothes, to let my hair go, to wear some makeup." She waved a hand down her length, indicating the teal-blue capri pants with small beads dangling from the bottom and the matching top with a mandarin collar and capped sleeves.

Jesse pointed to Beth's teal sandals. "You've even painted your toenails orange. You've never done that before."

"Jane helped me pick out the color."

Jesse's mouth fell open.

"The guys are looking at us funny. We'd better take the food to them." Beth left her friend by the back door and walked toward Samuel and Nick by the grill.

Her date's eyes glittered dark fire as they roamed over her. She nearly stumbled, and had to catch herself before she sent the platter with their dinner flying across the deck.

With warm humor Samuel winked at her, taking the platter from her. "Is everything all right with Jesse?"

Nick glanced back at his wife. "I think you two foiled her plans for the evening."

Samuel placed his arm about her shoulders. "That's too bad. What plans?"

Beth marveled at how innocent he looked. She pressed her lips together to keep her laugh inside while Nick forked the top steak and flipped it onto the grill.

"You don't know that—" Nick studied Samuel for a long moment. "You do know."

Both of them nodded as Jesse joined the group, carrying the corn on the cob wrapped in aluminum foil.

"Okay, now that you all have had some fun with me, I have to say, Beth, I do like your new look."

"Who says we're having fun with you?" Samuel drew Beth even closer and gazed into her eyes. "I like your new look *and* your old look."

Her stomach flip-flopped, her legs going weak. Samuel's grip on her tightened as she began to sink from the sensations his look sent through her. "I have to admit I like this outfit, too. Your daughter has great taste."

"Jane went with you shopping for clothes, too?" Jesse handed the corn to Nick.

"Yes."

"I'm surprised I didn't hear anything about it. That would have been hard to keep quiet in Sweetwater."

Beth grinned. "That's why we went to Lexington to shop. I didn't want the gossip hounds to work overtime."

"Believe me, when they see you, their tongues will be wagging, unless this is the extent of your new wardrobe."

"No. I bought several outfits. The next one I'm wearing to church tomorrow and the third one to school on Monday."

"Are they all like this one?" Jesse asked Samuel.

"I don't know. I couldn't get my own daughter to tell me what Beth bought. I have to wait with the rest of you."

Jesse planted her hands on her waist. "Beth

Coleman, you've always been an open book. I can't believe you are keeping secrets from us."

"And loving every minute of it."

Nick turned the steaks over. "Jesse will be up all night speculating."

The scent of grilling meat and spring flowers mingled to lace the air. Beth backed up until she felt the lounge chair and sat. "You'll just have to make the best of it, Nick. I'm sure you'll think of something to keep yourselves entertained while losing sleep."

Jesse burst out laughing.

"By the way, where are the kids?" Beth asked, observing Samuel moving around the chair to stand behind her. Her pulse quickened in anticipation of his touch.

"Cindy and Nate are at Gramps's, for the whole night."

Finally—an eternity later, in Beth's mind—Samuel settled his hands on her shoulders. Since she had come up with the scheme to give Jesse what she wanted—Beth and Samuel together as a couple—he had thrown himself wholeheartedly into the role of her boyfriend. She had thought it would be easier than fighting all the attempts by her friend to get them together. She was having second thoughts. She enjoyed his touch too much, and since they had arrived she had felt more and more comfortable with his arm around her or his hand on her.

"Jesse has gone back inside," Beth whispered, standing out in front of her friend's house, the stars shining bright in the dark sky, the night air cool but pleasant, especially with Samuel's arm around her shoulders, his warmth seeping into her to ward off any chill. "You don't have to pretend any longer."

"Pretend?"

"You know, that we're a couple. Jesse isn't looking."

"She could be spying out one of her windows as we speak."

"She isn't. I think we have convinced her we're an item, and tomorrow the whole town will know."

"I think the whole town already thinks that."

"They do?"

"Yeah. Yesterday Liz asked Aunt Mae when I was planning to propose."

Beth pulled away and squared off in front of him on the sidewalk, her hands going to her waist. "Propose! We've only been on two dates."

"Three."

"Okay. Three. Honestly, the people of Sweetwater are getting worse than Jesse ever was."

Samuel took her hands and stepped closer until little was between them, not even air. "They care about you. They want to see you happy. I think that's sweet."

"You don't have to be married to be happy. I've been happy for the past thirty-eight years without a man. I've been—"

He lowered his head toward hers, cutting off the flow of her words. "I'm going to kiss you. I just wanted to warn you."

She nodded, a slight movement before his lips crushed down onto hers. The kiss stole her breath and any rational thought she had left. Standing on her tiptoes, plastered against him, she felt transported to a realm of the senses where she focused on his smallest detail—the dimple in his left cheek, the citrus aftershave he wore, the lines at the corners of his eyes that deepened when he smiled, the gruffness of his voice, the rough texture of his hands that he built things with. She had all those little traits memorized so that she could instantly recall him when he wasn't around.

When he drew back, resting his forehead

on hers, she realized that he was as affected as she was by their kiss. She imagined if she laid her palm over his heart she would feel it beating as fast as hers was.

"That wasn't for the benefit of anyone but you," he whispered in the stillness.

Desperate to get control of her careening emotions, she backed away and glanced around her. "Thank goodness it's late."

"Yes, and I suppose we both need to get home. I have a sermon to deliver twice tomorrow." He took her hand and began to walk toward her street.

"After the meal Jesse prepared for us, I'm glad we're walking home."

"And it gives me a little more time with you. Private time without others around."

"Are you talking about Allie earlier this evening riding her bike alongside us as we walked over to Jesse's?"

"Not quite what someone would expect on a third date, but Allie was dying to come along and see you. I think she's jealous that Jane steals so much of your time when you're over at our house. Allie even told me the other day she needed tutoring."

"She does? I thought she got all A's."

"She had one B on her report card last

time. I think she'll survive, but she said it right after you and Jane returned from Lexington."

"I'll try and plan something special with just me and her."

"You don't have to, Beth." His grasp on her hand tightened, drawing her closer to his side as they walked.

"I want to. Allie is so sweet. She reminds me of my sister when she was that age."

"And Jane reminds you of yourself?"

"There are similarities."

"Then my oldest daughter should be just fine when she grows up." Samuel paused at an intersection, looking up and down the street before crossing.

"She's almost grown up, Samuel. It won't be long before she's eighteen and heading for college."

"I know, I know. I'm not sure I'm going to like that change."

"I'm beginning to appreciate change in my life. For so many years I tried very hard to keep everything status quo. Now I'm learning to embrace change."

"Hence the new clothes and look?"

"Yes, as well as the plans to go to Brazil." She had to mention her plans. She had to ground not just him but herself in what was going to come in less than two months. She'd made a commitment to herself and the Christian Mission Institute. She didn't back down from her commitments.

Samuel turned up her oak-lined street. "What are you going to do about your house?"

"I'm keeping it. It's finally paid for. If my sister or brothers want to come back to Sweetwater, they'll have a place to stay."

"What about renting it out?"

"I don't know. I would like a place myself to come home to between assignments." She couldn't even explain to herself why she wasn't doing something with her childhood home. She envisioned herself coming back to Sweetwater from time to time to renew friendships and ground herself in the place she had come from, before heading back out into the world.

"Who's going to look after it while you're gone?"

She stopped on the sidewalk that led to her house. "You're full of questions tonight. I haven't come up with anyone yet. Any suggestions?"

"I will."

"I can't ask you—"

He brushed his fingers over her lips. "You didn't ask. I volunteered. Just as you did to tutor Jane. Let me do this for you. My house is almost back to normal, thanks to you. Jane's happier than I've seen her in a long time. I think that's your influence on her. I don't have to argue with her to get her to study. She wants to. Maybe I should ask what you have done with my daughter."

She wanted his fingers back whispering across her lips. This evening his touch had become so natural to her, as though he had been doing it for years. But she had to put a halt to the direction her thoughts were going. Dangerous territory. "I'm glad Jane is settling in. She's forming some good friends at school, and Ryan is a wonderful young man."

"I have to agree. Jane even spent the night at a friend's house last night. She's talking on the phone to her friends here in Sweetwater. She's laughing, smiling more. I'm beginning to feel the town puts something in the water. My children haven't been happier."

"We're a close community. We take care of each other."

"That's apparent all the time. When we need help at the church, there's always someone to do it. Usually more than one person. Our outreach fund is healthy."

"Speaking of the outreach fund, how's the dollhouse coming for the Fourth of July auction?"

"I should be finished very soon. If I get some time this week, I'll show you the completed house next weekend. Then the real fun begins—making the furniture, the odds and ends for the place. It'll be a family project."

"I'd love to help. I used to love playing with my dolls when I was growing up. It'll bring back fond memories."

Samuel started up the walk to Beth's house, again reaching out and clasping her hand. "You've got yourself a deal. I know Saturdays can be busy. We could work on it on Sunday afternoons after church. I can usually corral my kids then."

The thought of doing the project with his family brought a smile to Beth's mouth. She'd missed her own family since Daniel had left for college in January. For years she had wondered what it would be like to be free of raising children. She'd made plans for that time, but hadn't really figured on how lonely it could be by herself in her now large house without three siblings. Once she was in Brazil, she would have plenty of people around her at the mission and a new life to learn.

"Then I'll pencil you and your family in for the next few Sundays." Beth stopped at the bottom of the steps that led to her porch and faced Samuel.

He took both her hands in his, bringing them up between them. "You should stay for dinner afterward. That's the least we can do for your help."

"I'd love to."

"Well, then, I guess this is good night." He began to lean toward her, hesitated, then pulled back. He squeezed her hands, then spun about and left.

Beth watched him walk away, already missing his company. He was such a good man that maybe after she was gone Jesse could find someone for him. But when she thought about Samuel dating someone else, jealousy, something she rarely felt, sprang forth, surprising her. Maybe she wouldn't say anything to Jesse.

"Close your eyes." Samuel clasped Beth's hand to lead her into his workshop in the basement.

The scent of sawdust and paint hung in the air as she stepped through the doorway, confident that Samuel wouldn't run her into a wall or table.

"You can open your eyes now."

When she did, the first thing she saw was a modern split-level house sitting on the workbench, painted as though it was made of light brown stones with dark brown trim. "I love it!"

"I started to do a Victorian house like Allie's, but I wanted it to be as unique as Allie's, so I went with something more updated."

"It's beautiful. You could be a carpenter."

"It worked for Jesus, but I think I'll keep my day job. I'm enjoying what I'm doing again."

"Good. I'm glad to hear that. I know you were having your doubts, but as I told you before, your congregation doesn't feel you're doing a bad job at all." Beth moved closer to get a better look at the house. "You've got a deck and a hot tub. You really have gone modern."

"Do you think it will do well at the auction?"

"I can think of several people who will bid

on it. Jesse will want it for Cindy and I bet Zoey will want it, too."

"I was thinking next of doing a farmhouse or a New England saltbox house. What do you think?"

"You should ask the people who will be lined up after the auction what they want, because I believe the ones who bid and don't get the split-level house will want you to do one for them. Your dollhouse is going to rival Jesse's dolls."

"It's just a hobby."

"That may be so, but it won't stop people from knocking at your door." She straightened from inspecting the different rooms. "What do you want to start with first?"

"I'll leave that decision up to you and the kids."

"Where are they?"

"Jane should be here soon. She went home with a friend after church. Allie's out back playing and Craig's picking up his room again. The first time he managed to get sidetracked and only put away one thing."

"Ah, I remember those days. With Daniel I finally had to shut the door and not go into his room—otherwise we would have been fighting all the time. I had more important battles to fight with him, like graduating from high school." Her gaze swept the neat workshop, all his tools in a certain place. "Where's Aunt Mae?"

"In the kitchen making a dessert for dinner. She was glad you agreed to stay and eat. She loves to make desserts, but only does it when we have company."

As Beth started for the stairs that led to the first floor, Samuel placed his hand at the small of her back and walked next to her as though they were back on Jesse's deck trying to make a point with her friend. For a few seconds his nearness robbed Beth of any coherent thought.

Then she realized he had asked her a question. "I'm sorry. What did you say?"

"Which room are we going to start with?"

"The den. That's the family room, the most important room in the house."

Climbing the stairs, she was aware of Samuel behind her and was glad she'd worn her new white slacks with a bright lime-green cotton shirt. No more dull shades for her. She was really getting into wearing all different colors. She figured she'd blend in with the vivid birds of the Amazon.

Samuel directed Beth to his den while he

rounded up the rest of the family. She crossed to the large window overlooking the backyard and saw Allie playing in her fort at one end of the swing set. She was an adorable child. Beth could remember wishing, when she had been in her late twenties and early thirties, that she'd given birth to a baby as her friends had. But when she'd turned thirty-five she'd given up that dream and replaced it with seeing something other than Sweetwater.

What would have happened if Samuel had entered her life five years before? she wondered as Allie jumped down from the fort and ran toward the back door.

Turning away from the window, Beth drew in a deep breath and smelled the scent of an apple pie baking. Her mouth watered in anticipation of the dessert Mae was preparing. Beth didn't make desserts for herself. In fact, she didn't cook the way she used to love to when she had her siblings at home. She needed to cook more—it had always been good therapy for her when she had been stressed. The smells that saturated a kitchen were soothing to her—bread baking, coffee perking, meat sizzling, all kinds of spices like garlic and cinnamon.

Her stomach rumbled as the children began to file into the den, chattering, laughing, filling the house with warmth. What a nice way to spend Sunday, Beth thought, making her way to the two card tables that Samuel was setting up.

Mae hurried into the room, her apron still about her waist, some flour smudged on her cheek. "Are we ready to begin?"

Allie giggled. "You've got flour on you." She pointed toward her aunt's face.

"Oh, goodness me. And I have my apron still on. Be right back." For a large woman she moved quickly from the room.

"She's always forgetting to take off her apron. I don't even notice anymore." Samuel pulled a chair out for Beth to sit in.

She did and allowed him to push it toward the table. She felt his breath on her neck and shivered.

"I'm going to sit back and let you direct this show," he whispered into her ear.

She shivered again and turned slightly to glance back at him. Big mistake. His face was only inches from hers, and she could smell the mint of his toothpaste. She could remember their last kiss the week before. She leaned away, desperately trying to calm her riotous senses. "How did I get to be so lucky?"

He shrugged, straightening away from her. "Beats me. I just know I don't know the first thing about sewing."

"But you're going to make the furniture?"

"Yep. Craig and I will, just as soon as you all decide what you want in the house."

"I can paint the walls like I did for Allie's house," Jane said. "I already helped Dad with the outside stone."

"I should have known that was your work. Very realistic." Beth examined the floor plans that Samuel unrolled. "As I told your father, I think we should start with the den."

"It'll need a television and a couch like we have." Craig plopped down next to Jane.

Before long everyone joined in discussing what the room needed, and then moved on to what they would do next. Aunt Mae came back without her apron and with her face scrubbed clean and declared that the kitchen should be the next room to tackle after the den.

The conversation swirled around Beth. She listened to the children argue about what colors to use, then lifted her hands to signal quiet. When they didn't obey, she whistled, a high shrill one that immediately quieted everyone. They all looked at her, Allie's eyes round.

A smile danced in Jane's gaze. "She did that once in class. Got our attention real fast."

"I think you punctured my eardrum." Samuel rubbed his ear.

"That was something I learned when refereeing my siblings. It's very effective." Beth took a piece of paper and a pencil. "I think I need to assign jobs to each one of you or we'll never get anything done." She checked her watch. "We have been talking around and around for the past thirty minutes and not much has been settled."

Samuel relaxed back in his chair, his gaze trained on Beth as she dealt with his children and aunt, giving them each something to start on. She was in her teacher mode and he loved seeing her at work. She would be a terrific mother. He still couldn't believe a man hadn't seen past her defenses to the woman beneath. She was loving and caring, willing to give of herself. She would be good teaching at a mission. But he couldn't help wishing she wasn't leaving soon. He was afraid she would take part of his heart with her when she did go to Brazil. He was falling in love and didn't know how to stop the plunge.

* * *

The sunlight streamed through the branches of the maple tree and crisscrossed a pattern over the stones in the path. Beth watched the light dance about as the warm spring breeze blew the branches. Everything had come to a grinding halt today, and she didn't know how to deal with it.

Going to the doctor for her physical before she traveled to Brazil was supposed to have been routine, not a big deal. Now it was. She could still remember her doctor telling her this morning after she had reviewed the results from the mammogram she'd had a few days before, "We need to do a needle biopsy. I'm scheduling you for the procedure Monday morning. If it's malignant, we'll need to operate right away."

She hadn't heard much of what the doctor had said after she'd uttered the word, *malignant*. All Beth's fears rushed through her like a raging river. Hugging her arms to her, she tried to still the tremors, but they racked her body.

She was going to leave in five weeks. If the lump was malignant, she wouldn't be able to. She— Beth couldn't think beyond that. She buried her face in her hands and desperately tried to keep the tears inside.

It might not be. She had to hold on to that hope. She had to put her faith in the Lord that He knew best.

"Beth? Are you out here?"

She lifted her head, forcing a smile to her lips, swallowing the tears lumped in her throat. She didn't want to worry Samuel with the news the doctor had given her, especially since there was a good chance nothing was really wrong. "Yes, by the pond."

Samuel appeared on the stone path, dressed in black slacks and a white knit shirt. He returned her grin with one of his own, which dimpled his left cheek and crinkled his eyes. "I was just thinking about you."

"You were?"

"Yeah. I knew you went to the doctor today. How did it go?"

The smile on her lips wavered, and it took a supreme effort on her part to keep it in place. "Fine. Fit as a fiddle." *Unless you consider the lump I have in my breast,* she added silently, not wanting to tell Samuel unless she absolutely had to. His wife had died from breast cancer. She was afraid what the news would do to him. She would protect him as long as possible.

Samuel settled on the bench next to her. "I wonder where that saying came from. I never thought of a fiddle as being fit."

She shrugged, latching on to the inane topic of conversation to keep her mind off what she didn't want to think about. "I haven't the faintest idea. A lot of sayings don't make sense." But for the life of her she couldn't come up with a single one at the moment.

"I have to admit some things in life don't make sense."

She leaned away from him and stared into his face. "Are we going to get into a big philosophical discussion?"

"We could take our government for starters. Some of the red tape is senseless. Or how about—"

She stopped his words with her fingertips, much as he had done to her in the past. "I make it a practice not to discuss politics with anyone."

The feel of his lips against her fingers sent a shock wave through her body. Not a smart move. She shifted her hand.

"Okay. Let's talk about the end of the

school year. We need to plan a party for our graduating seniors. Do you think you're up to doing that?"

"No," she replied before she realized what she was saying.

"No? Are you ill? I think that's the first time I've heard you say no."

"I'm going to be so busy the next few weeks I'm afraid I might not do the party justice. See if Zoey will." She wasn't lying to her minister, just not elaborating on what she meant by busy.

"Zoey would be good. I'll do that. I know in the past the seniors have been honored at a church service, and I still want to do that, but I would also like to do something special for them after the service. Graduating from high school is a big deal."

Beth saw Samuel's lips moving as he spoke, but for the life of her she couldn't focus on what he was saying. She kept going over what the doctor had told her and the implications of having breast cancer—what it would mean to her, to her plans for the future, to Samuel when he heard the news.

She clenched her teeth to keep from asking Samuel to pray for her. She couldn't do that to him—not to the man she loved. The revelation snatched her breath away, causing her to gasp.

"What's wrong?" Samuel asked in mid-sentence as he twisted around and stared at her, his sharp gaze honing in on her as though he was delving inside her mind to read her innermost thoughts.

Chapter Ten

Panic mingled with stunned bemusement. This was a secret Beth didn't want Samuel to know, especially if she did have breast cancer. She didn't want him to relive his past. Even though he didn't love her as he had his wife, he was a caring man who would feel for her if she had cancer and it would be pure agony for him. She wanted to spare him for as long as she could.

"Nothing a little rest won't take care of," she finally said. "Even though I didn't teach today, having a physical is exhausting work. All that poking and prodding. And of course, the worst is the fasting for the blood work." Beth waved her hand in the air in a flippant manner meant to dismiss the subject, and prayed that Samuel would take the hint.

"Have you eaten since the doctor's?" Samuel asked, looking at her closely, his eyes dark pinpoints.

"No, and I guess I should."

He rose in one fluid motion. "You certainly should eat. It's lunchtime. I'm taking you to Alice's Café. Do you have to get back to school?"

"No, I took the whole day off because I wasn't sure how long the physical would take."

"Good. Then let's go." He tugged on her hand to assist her to her feet.

Short of telling him what was wrong, Beth didn't see any way of getting out of having lunch with Samuel. On a normal day she would be happy to share a meal with him. But today wasn't normal. She needed to think, to make some plans, to pray.

"But I have to warn you I'm really not very hungry." Fear knotted her stomach into such a tight ball she was afraid anything she did eat would come right back up.

"Don't let Alice hear you say that."

"You're right. Maybe I should just go home. I wouldn't want to upset Alice."

Samuel stopped on the stone path and faced her. "Are you sure you're all right?"

Her panic mushroomed. She couldn't out-and-out lie to Samuel, and yet she couldn't tell him what was really wrong. She didn't want to see that look on his face when he heard she might have cancer.

He covered her forehead with his hand. "Maybe you're coming down with something."

"It's springtime. My allergies have been acting up. I'm stuffed up. I think after a good nap I'll feel much better." She skirted him on the path and started for her car in the parking lot.

He caught up with her. "Aunt Mae has a great chicken soup I can bring over later."

"Does chicken soup really work?"

"Aunt Mae swears by it."

"Sure. I'll see you later." She hurriedly climbed into her car before he asked any more questions.

Hopefully by the evening she would have her act together enough to get the chicken soup and send him on his way. Until she knew what she would have to deal with she would avoid seeing Samuel. A certain look would probably have her clinging to him for support. She couldn't do that to him, not after the ordeal he had gone through with his wife.

* * *

"I can't say anything to him." Beth stood at the window overlooking the high school parking lot, watching the rain fall in gray sheets. Dismal. The weather reflected her mood.

Zoey approached Beth and placed a hand on her shoulder. "You need to. He cares about you and he should know."

"I just can't! Right now I couldn't handle the look of fear that will appear in his eyes when he hears I was diagnosed with breast cancer, that I'm going in to have the lump removed tomorrow."

"He will hear, Beth. You can't keep this a secret. Your students will know you're gone. Jane is in your class."

"I haven't told them anything, and certainly nothing about having cancer."

"Still, Jane will tell him you weren't at school. Look at the chicken soup he brought over when you were having problems with your allergies."

Beth let her head sag forward, the tension in her neck shooting down her back and shoulders. "I know."

"He'll call your house and get your answering machine. Then he'll begin to worry, especially when you aren't at school the next day. Do you want him to go through that?"

Beth balled her hands into tight fists until her fingernails dug into her palms. "No! I want to spare him any grief. That's why I haven't said anything yet." *Even though I would love to have him hold me and tell me everything will be all right.* Her reeling emotions made her stomach constrict into a cold knot.

Rubbing her hands up and down her arms to ward off a bone-deep chill, she turned away from the rain-soaked landscape and faced her friend. "Will you tell him tomorrow for me? After I've gone into surgery?"

"Beth, you have never been a coward before. You need to tell him yourself tonight."

Tears blurred her eyes, and Zoey's face wavered in front of her. "It's too much. My cup is full."

The fear Beth had held pushed down in the dark recesses of her mind blossomed into a full-blown panic. *What if the doctor doesn't get all the cancer? What if it has spread to the lymph nodes? What if I only have a few months to live? What if...*

She squeezed her eyes shut, trying to keep the tears inside, but they leaked out, rolling down her face. "I've left everything in order in my room. A sub shouldn't have a problem. I—" Beth choked on the words lodged in her throat. She rushed past Zoey, paused at her office door and added, "Please tell him for me. I can't, Zoey. I can't do that to him."

Outside her friend's door Beth glanced up and down the hallway, relieved that it was empty. With tears flowing, she hurried to her classroom and grabbed her purse, sweater and umbrella. When she paused on the top step at the front of the school, she stared into the grayness that blanketed the parking lot and fought back the panic that had descended in Zoey's office.

She had so much to do that evening. She had to call each of her siblings and talk to them. No, she would wait to tell them later. But she did have to tell Darcy, Jesse and Tanya. She had to— The cold knot in the pit of her stomach grew. Shuddering, she slid the umbrella open and made a dash for her Jeep.

Do not think, Beth.

Do not think, Beth.

She kept chanting that sentence over and over in her mind to keep it blank of all thoughts.

Ten minutes later she arrived home to an empty, silent house. She immediately flipped on the television and turned it up loud. The noise that permeated the rooms kept the worry at bay for a few minutes while she changed her clothes and began to prepare for the next day. Then the doubts and fears came back in full force, sending her to her knees in the middle of her bedroom, a set of pajamas for the hospital clasped in her hand.

Lord, I don't know where to begin. I feel so lost and alone. Why cancer? Why now? I wanted to help people in other parts of the world. I had everything planned out. I would do Your work. Now I'm fighting for my life and so scared. Please show me what You want. Please help me.

Beth folded over, burying her face in her hands and going to the floor. What little control she'd thought she had over her life had been snatched away. The terror, the emptiness crashed down on her.

Through the sound of people talking on the television she heard the insistent ringing of her bell. She tried to ignore it, but the person at her front door wouldn't go away. The noise kept up, echoing through her mind, declaring that the outside world would not leave her alone to wallow in self-pity.

Beth rolled to her feet and trudged toward the front door, opening it without even checking who was ringing her bell, because she was so sure it was Zoey or one of her other three friends, come to talk some sense into her.

Instead, Samuel stood on her porch, his hair wet from the rain, rivulets of water running down his face. Worry darkened his eyes. Had Zoey told him already?

Please don't let it be that, Lord. I can't deal—

"Beth, what's wrong?" he shouted over the loud noise.

"Nothing." *Except that I have breast cancer. Don't look at me like that.* When he glanced toward the living room where the television was, she added, "I was in the other room and wanted to hear the show." She hoped he didn't ask which show, because she had no idea what was on at the moment or even what channel she had flipped on. That hadn't mattered at the time—she'd needed voices to fill the silence of the house.

"May I come in?" he asked, because she still blocked his entrance into her house.

No. "Sure." She stepped to the side, gripping the edge of the door so tightly that her knuckles whitened. Peering down at her casual attire, stained with paint and ripped in a few places, she said, "I wasn't expecting any guests."

He arched a brow. "'Guest' sounds so formal. I thought we were more than that."

A shaft of lightning brightened the dim foyer, followed almost immediately by a boom of thunder. "What brings you out on a night like this? If I didn't have some…housework to do, I'd be cuddled up on the couch reading a good book."

He combed his fingers through his damp hair, then rubbed the back of his neck. "I don't know. I just had an urge to see you. Is everything all right?"

How could he know something was wrong? I've been so careful not to give anything away.

Her heart seemed to come to a standstill. A tight band about her chest constricted her breathing. She masked her tension by moving past Samuel and into the living room to switch off the television that was now irritating.

"Beth?"

She spun around and pasted a smile on her face. "What could be wrong other than I have too many papers to grade and so I can't curl up on the couch and read a good book?"

"I thought you had housework to do."

"I do, then papers to grade." *It wasn't a lie,* she said silently, to soothe her conscience. She did have a few things to do around the house because she wouldn't be here for a couple of days—like watering her plants, the ones that had managed to live through the winter, and...well, that was all, but still, that chore was considered housework. She flipped her hand toward a stack of papers, most of them graded. "Those await me. So what could possibly be wrong that time won't take care of?" She managed to say the last sentence without strangling on the words, but she slid her gaze away as though immensely interested in those few papers that still needed grading.

Samuel searched her living room with his eyes, the whole time massaging his nape. "I don't know what came over me. I..." He raised his broad shoulders in a shrug.

Tell him, a little voice said inside her head.

"I guess I've been more edgy lately."

"Why?" she quickly asked, desperately wanting to center the conversation about him.

"In a few days it will be the third anniversary of Ruth's death. It's always been hard on me."

The tightness in her chest expanded. How could she add to his pain, especially at a time like this?

Chicken. You should be the one to talk to him about it, that inner voice taunted. *Not Zoey.*

But when Beth stared into his dark eyes and saw pain reflected in their depths, she knew she wouldn't say a word. Not tonight. Later she would explain her reluctance, because she knew she couldn't keep it a secret for much longer—not in Sweetwater. She loved her hometown, but this was definitely a downside to the town. Everyone knew everything eventually.

"I'm so sorry, Samuel. Losing a loved one is never easy. I wish I could help make it better for you."

He covered the distance between them. "Your presence in my life—our lives—has made it easier, Beth. Thank you."

Her fragile emotions threatened to come apart at his words. With his hair slightly tousled and wet from the rain, he looked adorable. She concentrated on the turned-up corners of his mouth and wished she could sample another kiss. She backed away before acting on her wish. That would only complicate an already complicated situation.

"I appreciate you coming over to check on me, but as you can see I'm perfectly fine." She spread her arms wide.

"You aren't gonna send a poor guy out into the driving rain without at least one cup of hot coffee?"

The hopeful gleam in his eyes unraveled her resolve to send him on his way as quickly as she could. "I guess I could take a break from…my housework for *one* cup of coffee."

He grinned. "You make the best in Sweetwater. Thanks!"

She didn't want to blush at his blatant compliment, but she felt the heat singe her cheeks and knew she had. She hurried toward the kitchen to put on some coffee.

"I thought you always had a pot on when you were here."

"I forgot when I came home." The way she was feeling she was lucky she'd made it home. "It won't take long to brew. Have a seat."

Samuel settled into a chair at the table as

though he was at home in her kitchen. They had grown close over the past four months, beyond friendship, and yet all there really could be between them was friendship.

To keep busy she rifled through her cabinets until she found some chocolate cookies. "I know these are store bought, but they are very good. Want any?"

"Sure."

Beth withdrew several and placed them on a plate, then put it on the table in front of Samuel. When the coffee finished perking, she poured them each a cup and brought the sugar bowl to him.

He doctored his coffee with only one spoonful of sugar. "I can't totally give up the sweetness, but I'm working on it."

She cupped the mug between her hands and savored the warmth emanating from it. Even though it was spring outside and not chilly, she felt cold deep down inside her. "I told Jesse about the dollhouse and she is dying to see it. I told her she had to wait until the auction like everyone else."

"Good. I want to propose a prison ministry using our outreach funds. When I go to see Tom, I see so many inmates who need the Lord's guidance."

"Has anything happened with Tom?"

He shook his head, then took a long sip. "At least he's seeing me now."

"Tanya's resigned to the divorce, but she hasn't said anything to Crystal yet."

"She needs to tell her soon. Word will get out, and it's best for her to hear it from her mother."

Beth dropped her gaze to a spot halfway between them on the oak table. "She'll tell her when the time's right."

"For who?"

"Tanya. She's had to deal with a lot lately." She realized she was really talking about herself. She should be the one to talk to Samuel about her cancer, but she couldn't get the words past her lips.

"But she's not alone. God's with her and we're with her."

"Do you really feel that way?"

He looked her directly in the eye and said, "Yes. Two months ago I wouldn't have agreed, but you've made me see so much that I was refusing to see. The Lord has been with me the whole time. Just because a person prays to God doesn't mean that what he prayed about will happen. The Lord knows best, not me. I'd forgotten that."

Does He? For a few seconds her faith wavered. Then she remembered a verse from Romans. "And we know that all things work together for good to them that love God, to them who are the called according to His purpose," she murmured.

Her hand trembled as she placed her mug on the table. *Tell him,* that inner voice pleaded.

She stared at his handsome face, the words rising within her. She opened her mouth to tell him, but as before nothing would come out. Quickly she lifted the mug again and sipped at her coffee. She could handle only so much, and telling him wasn't one of those things. Not yet.

Samuel stepped off the elevator and immediately saw Zoey pacing in front of the nurses' station. He headed for her, concerned by the worried look in her eyes. "Aunt Mae didn't tell me who was in the hospital. One of your children?"

"No." She waved him toward a waiting room across from the nurses' station, then preceded him.

When he entered the room, his gaze swept over Zoey, Darcy, Tanya and Jesse, and he knew who was in the hospital: Beth. The thought that she might be hurt slammed through him as though a truck had run over him. "What's wrong with Beth?" His question came out in a gruff whisper, but then, he was amazed his voice even worked.

"She's in surgery right now." Zoey peered toward Jesse for support, then back at Samuel. "She has breast cancer. The doctor is removing the lump."

He sank into a chair not far from him, his legs giving out. His throat closed, cutting off his air until it was difficult even to breathe. "Breast cancer," he managed to choke out, while the pressure in his chest squeezed his heart until it felt as though it were splitting into fragmented pieces.

"Yes, she found out a few days ago and the doctor wanted to operate right away." Jesse came forward. "We wanted her to tell you. She couldn't. She asked Zoey to."

Four pairs of eyes were on him, their own pain mirrored in their gazes. He couldn't look at them any longer. He dropped his head, staring unseeingly at his lap, his hands twisting together, their outline blurring.

No, not again, Lord. Why Beth? Why me?
Silence greeted his plea.

The sounds of the regional hospital cut into the quiet in his mind—beeping noises, people talking outside the waiting room, a doctor being called over the intercom system. He tried to draw air into his lungs, but a tightness gripped his chest. Light-headed, he finally looked up at the four women still staring at him, the worry on their faces now evolving into full-fledged concern.

Over three years ago he had lived through this very scene, only to lose his wife in the end because the cancer had spread so quickly. Again he took a breath, this time managing to fill his lungs partially.

Zoey sat next to him and placed her hand on his arm. "I'm so sorry. I tried to get Beth to tell you yesterday, but she said she couldn't handle it. She was still trying to deal with the fact she had cancer. Everything moved so fast once they discovered the malignant lump."

"How long has she been in surgery?" Why hadn't she been able to turn to him? He had failed her when she needed him most.

"A while. It shouldn't be much longer."

He should have been here from the beginning, but he had been out running when Zoey had called the house. He'd come as soon as he could after his aunt had told him Zoey needed him at the hospital, that she would be on the second floor in the waiting room. He should have held Beth and prayed with her last night, but instead he had sat in her kitchen drinking her coffee, talking about unimportant things, oblivious to what was really going on in her head. In his heart he'd known something was wrong, but when she hadn't said anything he hadn't pushed. He should have pushed.

For the next twenty minutes he paced the length of the room, counting his steps because he didn't want to think about what was going on with Beth. If he could numb his mind, he would be all right.

"I'm getting some coffee. Do you want any?" Darcy asked everyone.

"I could use a cup." Tanya started to lift her purse from the floor.

Samuel stopped his pacing and said, "I'll get the coffee, and it's on me."

Pivoting, he hurried from the room and went in search of the vending machine on the floor. Out in the corridor he felt as though he could breathe a little more easily without Beth's friends watching him as if they were waiting for him to explode. He had to hold himself together long enough to find out if

Beth would be all right. He'd lost control once before in his life and had hurt his family in the process. He couldn't do that again, and if that meant shutting down his feelings concerning Beth, then that would be what he had to do. She had become too important to him. He would be there as her friend, but that was all. Emotionally he couldn't afford anything else.

After selecting three coffees from the vending machine, Samuel headed back to the waiting room. Approaching the group of women, he noticed a man in their midst talking to them. He rushed forward, realizing the doctor was reporting on Beth.

Smiling, Zoey looked at him. "She's going to be okay."

"I removed the lump," the doctor said. "The cancer was contained and hadn't spread to the lymph nodes."

Relief made Samuel's hand tremble as he handed the paper cups to Tanya and Darcy. "Can we see her now?"

"She's still in recovery, but I'll have the nurse tell you when she's back in her room." The doctor left the waiting room.

Jesse grabbed her purse and rummaged inside. "I'll call her sister and brothers now."

"Why aren't they here?" Samuel asked, swallowing some of the bitter, lukewarm coffee. He winced and realized he'd forgotten the sugar that Beth was trying to wean him from.

"Beth didn't want them to come home for this. She made me promise not to call until after the operation." Jesse retrieved her cell phone and a slip of paper with some phone numbers on it. She walked to the other end of the room and began making her calls.

"I guess we're lucky she told us." Zoey went to the phone in the waiting room and began punching in some numbers as she continued, "I'm calling the school to let the secretary know what's going on."

Now that he knew Beth was going to be all right, anger started festering inside him. Beth shouldn't have kept something like this a secret—not from him. Didn't the past few months mean anything to her? He'd begun to think he meant something to her, but that was obviously not the case. Beth had told only her closest friends, and he hadn't been one of them. Her rejection hurt, fueling his anger.

"I'm going for a walk. I'll be back later," he told Beth's friends, and started for the door.

"What do we tell Beth when we see her? When will you be back?"

Samuel glanced over his shoulder and said to Zoey's questions, "I have no idea when, if ever."

He couldn't think in the hospital. He had to get away from it and try to make some sense out of his vacillating emotions.

"You told him?" Beth asked Zoey as her friend sat in the chair next to her bed.

"Yes."

Beth looked from Zoey to Jesse, then Darcy and Tanya. "Where is he?" Even though her mind was foggy from the anesthetic, concern for Samuel pushed to the forefront. She knew what the news would do to him and now she feared the worst.

"He went for a walk." Darcy glanced away from Beth as though she couldn't quite meet her eyes.

"What aren't you telling me?"

"Nothing," Jesse said too quickly.

"You don't have to protect me."

Jesse looked directly at Beth. "I'm not sure he's coming back."

Beth shouldn't have been surprised by the news and she wasn't, but disappointment that she wouldn't see Samuel flooded her. Despite not having the nerve to tell him about her cancer, she had still wanted to see him when she awakened from the operation. She loved her friends, but she needed Samuel. She needed to know he was all right. She needed him to tell her everything would be all right for her.

"I imagine this has brought back bad memories of his late wife." Beth plucked at the white cotton sheet, trying to keep her voice steady.

"He didn't look too well when I told him about you," Zoey murmured. "I don't think I did a very good job, either."

"Nonsense, Zoey. You did fine. It's not easy breaking that kind of news to anyone. I called your siblings." Jesse moved closer to the bed.

"They aren't coming, are they?" Beth didn't want her family descending on her, not when she felt so fragile—as if she would break at any moment. She needed to be alone, to lick her wounds by herself. Or even better, she needed Samuel.

"No, they're going to respect your wishes. But Holly said you'd better call her as soon as you can. Daniel is coming home in a few weeks to check on you. I couldn't reach Ethan because he is out of the country, but I left a message on his machine."

Beth tried to smile, but the corners of her mouth quivered. "Thanks, for calling them, Jesse. I'd forgotten that Ethan was on assignment in the Middle East for his newspaper."

Weariness slid over Beth, causing her to yawn. Her eyelids drooped, then snapped open.

"I think we'd better leave you to get some rest." Zoey rose from the chair and patted Beth's arm. "We're here for you and we will be when you get home. Anything you need just ask one of us or all of us." She leaned down and gave Beth a hug.

Each one embraced Beth and said she would pray for her. Then her four best friends left her alone to her thoughts. Where was Samuel now? What had she done to him?

Please, Lord, help him and heal any pain that my illness may have caused him. I don't ever want to hurt him. I love him too much.

As the prayer slipped through her mind, she closed her eyes and pulled the sheet and blanket up to her chin. Coldness pierced her as though she had been stabbed with an icicle. She burrowed down under the covers, sleep flowing over her....

A sound penetrated her sleep-drenched mind. She shifted on the bed, trying to get up, and pain spread outward from her chest. She remembered where she was and why. Her eyes bolted open to her dimly lit hospital room, darkness beyond the window. In the shadows stood a tall, muscular man she instantly recognized as Samuel. He stared out the window into the night, his body stiff, his hands curled into fists at his sides.

Her first thought was that he had come to see her. Then she really studied his stance and saw the anger barely contained, especially when he swung around and stabbed her with his icy look, much like the coldness earlier before she'd fallen asleep.

"I just wanted to make sure you were all right with my own two eyes." He started for the door.

"Please don't leave."

Chapter Eleven

Beth's plea went straight to Samuel's heart, twisting about it and squeezing. He halted but couldn't turn toward her, not yet when he was fighting both his anger and his pain. He'd tried to walk off his anger, and had thought he had succeeded until he found himself in her hospital room. Then all his fury had returned. While she'd slept, he'd watched, alternating between wanting to leave and stay.

Still facing the door, he said, "I don't think I'd be very good company at the moment."

"I'm sorry, Samuel. I couldn't bring myself to tell you what was happening to me."

He pivoted, having come back to discover one thing. "Are you really all right?"

"I'll be fine. Time's all I need. I had reconstructive surgery at the same time, so it will take me longer to get back on my feet, but I will get back on my feet. From what the doctor said they got it all."

"Good. Now I need to go." He took a step toward the door.

"Samuel, please."

Heaving a deep sigh, he swung back toward her again. "What do you want from me, Beth? I'm dealing with this the best way I can. You didn't think enough of me to include me in what was happening to you. That clearly tells me where we stand."

"That's not why I didn't say anything to you. I care too much, Samuel. I didn't want to be the one to hurt you any further. I know what you went through with Ruth. If I could have gone through this without you ever finding out, I would have. I knew that was impossible. Not in Sweetwater." Tears ran down her face and she did nothing to stop them.

The sight of the wet tracks on her cheeks tore through his defenses, but still he stayed by the door, not daring to go to her. She'd admitted she wouldn't have said anything to him if she had thought she could get away with it. That she thought so little of him drove the hurt even further into him. His emotions were shredded and he felt half a man at the moment. He couldn't help her until he helped himself. Part of him was grounded in what had happened in the past; the other was here with Beth trying to deal with feeling left out of an important part of her life, of feeling as though he had let her down by not being by her side through the whole ordeal from the very beginning.

He gripped the handle on the door and yanked it open. "I'll see you later."

Out in the corridor he drew in a shaky breath and looked down at his hands, spread in front of him. They trembled with the force of the intense emotions coursing through him. He knew of only one way to deal with what was going on inside him.

Samuel rode the elevator to the first floor and found the chapel. Inside the small, dimly lit room he sat on the pew before the altar, folded his hands together and prayed as he had never done before. He would not go back to the man he was three years ago. That time he had nearly been destroyed. And he knew he couldn't do this by himself.

Dear Heavenly Father, I believe You brought Beth into my life for a reason. She has helped me to find my way back to You, to heal the breach in my family. Please help her.

*Give me the knowledge to assist her through
her ordeal. Help me to overcome the pain
she caused when she didn't include me in her
life when she was hurting the most and
needed me the most.*

The serenity of the chapel seeped into his
soul and soothed away the hurt as though a
hand had reached inside him and stroked
away the pain. She was the best thing that
had happened to him in a long time. Thinking back to their discussions about Ruth, he
could see why she had excluded him and
faced her operation on her own. He had
opened up to her as he had to no one else, but
in so doing had put a barrier of fear between
them when she needed him most.

Now he could either walk away from her
or be there for her as a friend—anything beyond that he wasn't sure he was ready to
give.

The nurse had come in and closed the
blinds in Beth's room. The darkness beyond
her window invaded every corner. Beth
switched off all the lights except the night-
light near the bathroom and now lay in the
dimness, trying to gather her composure,
pull her life together. Even knowing Sam-

uel's reaction to her not telling him about the surgery and breast cancer, she didn't think she would have done anything differently. Remembering back to the evening before, she knew she couldn't have come up with the right words to ease his pain with her news. Maybe one day he would understand her motives for keeping quiet and having Zoey tell him.

She couldn't fight her feelings any longer. She loved him and that wasn't going to change or go away. But how could she compete with a ghost? His deceased wife was there between them.

She felt her tears return and determinedly squashed them. She had cried enough the past week—because of the cancer, because of her lost opportunity to go to Brazil, because of Samuel and what she had known she would do to him.

Her door swished open, and she turned her head to see who was coming into her room. Samuel stood just inside the entrance, a neutral expression on his face. He moved forward. Hope flared inside her as he made his way to her bed and sat in the chair next to her.

"It's dark in here. Were you trying to go to sleep?"

She shook her head, afraid to use her voice for fear it wouldn't work.

"Beth…" He took her hand and cupped it between his. "I'm sorry for getting angry earlier. I was purely reacting, not thinking. Can you forgive me?"

"If you'll forgive me for not having the courage to tell you myself. I wanted to. I…" She licked her dry lips and swallowed several times. "Will you hand me that glass of water on the stand?"

He reached for the peach plastic cup and gave it to her. "I won't kid you and tell you that you having breast cancer doesn't worry me because the doctor feels he got it all. In my head I know you'll be all right in time. In my heart I'll always worry about you. You're so special and very important to me."

Beth sipped her water, the cool liquid slipping down her parched throat. "That's the way I feel about you. In my head I knew I should have told you about my cancer, but in my heart I couldn't bring myself to do it. I tried. Really I did."

Leaning forward, he brushed his fingers across her moistened lips. "I know. It wasn't easy for Ruth to tell me either, and there had been no past history to contend with." When he settled back in the chair again, his hands clasped in his lap, he continued, "Now, let me make it up to you by having you come stay with us until you're back on your feet."

"I can't do—"

He held up his hand. "Shh. Yes, you can. Aunt Mae and I insist. Someone has got to take care of you for the next week or so. You didn't want your siblings to come home, so who is going to?"

Smoothing the blanket over and over, she murmured, "Me. I had planned to do it myself. I've taken care of myself for the past thirty-some years. This is no different."

"No. I won't let you do it by yourself. You need to be pampered and cared for, and I have a family who is eager to do it. I asked each one, and none of us will take no for an answer. At least consider staying with us for a few days. You've had major surgery. You shouldn't be by yourself."

Stunned by the invitation and the ardent way he asked, Beth found herself nodding, almost afraid not to from the look of determination on his face.

"Good. Then it's settled."

"You'll have to break the news to Zoey,

Darcy, Jesse and Tanya. I think they had planned on taking shifts staying with me."

"They can visit you at my house."

In all her adult life she had always been the one to pamper and take care of someone. She had never been the recipient before. She might go stir crazy before the first day was over, she thought. She wasn't very good at doing nothing.

With his arm about Beth, Samuel helped her to his bed while his three children and Aunt Mae filed into his bedroom behind him. "You're going to use my room."

"I can't kick you out of your own room."

"Yes, you can and besides, you don't have a say in this." Samuel assisted her as she eased onto his bed. "I've already set up my things downstairs in my office. There's a very comfortable couch that will be fine for me."

"But—"

He shook his head. "No buts. I didn't think it would be very restful to share a room with either a fifteen- or eight-year-old. And you need your rest."

"Yes, Dr. Morgan."

Even though he grimaced, a twinkle glinted

in his dark eyes. "I have a list of instructions from your doctor and I intend to carry out every last one of them."

"With our help," Allie chimed in.

Beth peered around Samuel and smiled at the young girl. "Thank you for letting me share your home."

"Dear, you're welcome anytime." Aunt Mae bustled over to the bed and began turning down the covers. "I think the best thing for you right now is to get some rest."

"That's all I've been doing the past few days. I've never had this much rest before."

"Have you ever been really sick or had an operation?" Aunt Mae fluffed up several king-size pillows and placed them against the cherry-wood headboard.

"No."

"Then you need to lie back and let us take care of you. I know what I'm doing and I'll make sure they do, too." The older woman tossed her head in the direction of Samuel and the children. "They really are very trainable."

"Aunt Mae!" Jane exclaimed, laughter in her voice.

Samuel's aunt grinned and winked. "Now, let's take off your shoes and get you comfortable."

Beth threw a "help me" look toward Samuel. He shrugged.

When Aunt Mae started to assist Beth with her shoes, Beth shook her head and said, "I can do it. Please, I'm not an invalid yet."

"Okay. Okay." The woman backed off. "I'll go prepare dinner, then. Come on, children, I need some help in the kitchen."

The three children left the room, grumbling the whole way. Allie even glanced back and started to say something to her father.

Samuel stopped her with his hand raised. "You go with Aunt Mae. You'll get to see Beth later." Then when the children had disappeared into the hallway, he turned back to her and added, "My family can be a bit overwhelming."

Beth thought about Allie, Craig, Jane and Aunt Mae and had to agree with Samuel, but their presence warmed her. They were overwhelming in a good way, reminding her of her siblings, who had filled her house with noise and laughter.

"I'm not sure you'll get the rest you need. I forgot about how much my children like you."

Beth slipped her shoes off and scooted back against the pillows, glad that she wore a comfortable jogging suit. "Good. They can keep me from being bored. I don't do lying around very well. Never had much of a chance, raising three siblings, so I don't even know if I can do it."

"You may regret saying that in a day or two. Allie already has a whole bunch of games she wants you to play with her."

"I might be able to work some on the dollhouse."

"We're almost done and remember, no work for you. That word shouldn't even be in your vocabulary for the next week or at least a few days."

"My, I'm seeing a whole new side to you."

He dragged a padded chair to the bed and sat. "The caring, wonderful side?"

She laughed. "Hardly. More like demanding, I'm-going-to-get-my-way-no-matter-what side."

Lines of merriment appeared at the corners of his eyes, fanning outward and adding a certain whimsical appeal to his charm. "Seriously, is there anything I can get you? Do you have everything you need from your house?"

"You and Zoey did a great job of packing what I needed." She pictured Samuel helping

Zoey gather her clothes and felt the heat of a blush sear her cheeks. Had he gone through her drawers and closet?

Samuel's gaze held hers for a long moment, penetratingly intense. "To put your mind at ease, Zoey wouldn't let me near your bedroom. I got the two books you wanted to read, your special blend of coffee and your address book with your stationary."

"Aunt Mae won't be offended because I brought my own coffee?"

"Not when she gets a taste of it. She'll be fighting me for a cup."

Now that she was settled, weariness washed over her. It was the middle of the afternoon. She never took naps, and yet she wanted one. She needed some coffee. "Speaking of my coffee, do you think I could get some?"

"Sure. But don't you think you should rest before dinner?"

Determined not to let her breast cancer change her life any more than it already had, she shook her head. "I don't believe in naps."

He levered himself out of the chair and hovered over her. "I'll go have Aunt Mae make some coffee and I'll share a cup with you. Then I insist you rest."

"Aye, aye, Captain."

He headed for the door. "You know I was a captain in the army."

The chuckle in his voice gave her a warm, cozy feeling as she let her eyelids close for just a moment. The scent of clean, fresh sheets teased her senses while she thought of the masculine decor in Sam-uel's room. Solid dark cherry-wood furniture with only a few knickknacks adorning the surfaces fit her image of Samuel. He was solid, like the pieces of furniture, with a no-nonsense personality. And yet, on the nightstand there was a picture of his family and a Bible, both important parts of his life.

The exhaustion she'd held back claimed her, whisking her away. She fought it, but for the life of her she couldn't pry her eyes open. Sleep blanketed her.

Samuel toed open his bedroom door, since his hands were occupied with holding two mugs of the delicious-smelling coffee that was Beth's special blend. Starting across the brown carpet toward his bed, he stopped halfway when he saw Beth with her head sagging to the side on the pillows propped against the headboard, her eyes closed in sleep. She looked beautiful and at peace even though she'd had a fright this past week. The doctor felt she would make a full recovery, and Samuel prayed the man was right, because staring at Beth in his bed, sleeping, made him realize how much he cared for her, that being her friend might not be enough.

Was it love? The kind that bound two people together forever?

Frowning, he covered the distance between them and placed her mug on a coaster on his nightstand. He caught a glimpse of the framed photograph of his family. Ruth smiled at him, her hands on Allie's shoulders. Looking at his deceased wife didn't bring the usual heartache and emptiness. Samuel glanced back at Beth, knowing she was the reason he was beginning to move on with his life, relishing again the fullness of it, especially his relationship with the Lord.

But would he be placing himself in a position to be hurt again if anything happened to Beth? What if the doctor was wrong? What if the cancer did return?

Easing onto the chair, he took a long sip of his coffee, relishing it as it slid down his throat. While he cupped the mug between his hands, he saw his wedding band on his left finger, the light gleaming in its golden depths. For the first time since he'd put it on over sixteen years ago, he was considering removing it and putting it away.

How would his children feel about him doing that?

Was he ready?

Was he in love with Beth?

Questions bombarded him as he stared at Beth in his bed. He sat drinking the rest of his coffee and watching her chest rise and fall gently as she slept. At peace. Safe.

By the time his mug was empty, Samuel knew he needed to move on. Even though his future with Beth was still very much up in the air, his first step was to take off his wedding band. Rising, he walked to his chest of drawers and pulled open the top one. With a twist he slipped the gold ring from his finger and placed it in a keepsake box.

Peering down at his bare finger, the skin where the ring had rested whiter than the rest of his hand, he waited for the feelings of guilt and sadness to inundate him. Instead, he experienced relief that he was finally moving forward in his life. Amazed, he turned toward Beth and discovered her watching him.

She screwed her face into a puzzled expression. "Are you all right?"

He nodded. "Better than I realized I would be."

Her frown deepened. "What do you mean?"

He held up his left hand. "I took off my wedding band."

Her eyes grew round. She sat up. "You did? Why?"

He strode to the chair and sat, placing his hands on his thighs, his fingers spread wide. "Because it was time. I was living in the past. That isn't good for me or my family."

"Sometimes telling ourselves what is good for us and really feeling that way are two different things."

"In my case, it isn't."

"We haven't talked about me having breast cancer. We've avoided the subject."

"And you don't want to avoid it any longer?"

"I think we need to talk about it. I know what your wife's illness did to you. I don't want to be the cause of any more pain for you."

Samuel leaned forward, sandwiching her hand between his. "I'm working on it. God and I have had some long talks lately." He hiked one corner of his mouth up. "I may not always see the big picture, but I'm trying. My main concern right now, Beth, is making sure you get back on your feet."

"If your aunt has any say, that may not be anytime soon."

"She loves to pamper, to do for others. Kinda reminds me of you."

Sadness entered Beth's expression. "I won't be able to go to Brazil in a few weeks like I had planned. The doctor said my recovery would be at least two and a half, three months." She slipped her hand free, plucking at the sheet. "I'll have to call the Christian Mission Institute to explain what happened. I hate letting anyone down."

"Most of all you?"

Her eyes gleamed with unshed tears. "I wanted to go. I have my passport. I'd bought some clothes for the jungle. I can't say my Portuguese was too great, but I am sure once I got there it would have improved. Now none of that makes any difference."

"Why do you say that? You could always leave later."

"The institute will have filled that position. They'll need someone to take my place."

"There are other positions, other groups."

Entwining the sheet about her hand, Beth shrugged. "I guess." When she brought her head up and looked him straight in the eye, she asked, "Do you think God is telling me I shouldn't leave Sweetwater?"

"That's something you have to work out with Him. I'm discovering He brought me to this town for a reason. Maybe it is to help Tanya or someone else. But the longer I am here, I know it in my heart." He patted his chest.

"How's Tanya really doing? I can tell something is wrong, but she wouldn't say what when she visited me that last time in the hospital."

"She received her divorce papers two days ago. She came to see me right after that. We prayed together."

"She should have said something to me."

"She didn't want to burden you."

She winced. "There's a lot of that going around."

"Then you understand her silence?"

"Yes." Beth straightened and reached for the phone. "But she isn't a burden. When will she realize that?" She punched in Tanya's number and waited for a good minute before hanging up. "No one's there. I'll call her later to check on her."

"I forgot. She's probably out at the farm. Crystal's riding again, with Darcy's help."

"Tanya agreed to that?"

"Crystal has been asking and asking for the past few months. Darcy has made sure that Crystal has the gentlest mare to ride."

"I have heard riding is good therapy."

"Conquering one's fears is important, too."

"Whose? Tanya's or Crystal's?"

"I think a little of both. The first time Crystal rode, Darcy told me she was white as a sheet and scared. She clenched the reins and hardly relaxed for the first twenty minutes. But by the end of the lesson she was laughing. This is the second time." He shifted in his chair. "We can learn something from Crystal."

"To meet our demons head-on?"

"Yep—she's quite a special young lady."

Beth blew out a long breath that lifted her bangs. "I'm out of commission for less than a week and look what happens. You know more about my friends and their lives than I do. Darcy didn't say a word."

"That's because the first lesson was yesterday evening."

"And they're out there again today?"

"Crystal got up this morning and insisted she go back this afternoon. Tanya couldn't say no and neither could Darcy."

She twisted her mouth into a frown. "What are they doing? Calling you every hour to give you updates?"

"Actually one of your group of friends does practically call me every hour to see how you're doing. I just ask them some questions to find out what's going on, so if you want to know I can tell you."

A smile graced her mouth. "I have some nice friends."

"Yes, you do, which says something about you."

Pink tinged her cheeks, adding some color to her pale features. She averted her face while stretching to grasp the mug. Fighting a yawn, she took a sip. "Even lukewarm this is good, and I need some caffeine if I want to stay up for dinner."

Standing, Samuel reached for her coffee and took it from her. "Take another nap. I'll bring you a tray when you're rested."

"But I don't want to be—"

"Don't, Beth. The best medicine for you is sleep. Aunt Mae's dinner can be heated up when you're ready to eat. I'll check back later."

She hid a yawn behind her hand. "I don't take naps, and certainly not two in one day."

"Then this is a good time to start the practice." He strode toward the door, opened it and glanced back to see Beth snuggle down under the covers.

He fought the urge to go back and tuck her in, as though that action would keep her safe. Her health was in the hands of the Lord now. God had brought Beth into his life for a reason. He needed to practice patience and see what the Lord had planned.

Allie clapped her hands. "I won! I won! Again!"

"You're one lucky girl," Beth said, shuffling the deck of cards.

"Can we play another game of war?"

"No, you can't, young lady. It's time for bed." Samuel entered the den and set a mug down next to Beth on the coaster on the coffee table.

She looked into it and frowned. "Milk?"

He stood next to his youngest. "You said you had a hard time falling asleep last night, so I thought this might help you. I hear warm milk is good right before bedtime."

Allie cocked her head to the side. "It's your bedtime, too?"

Tired, Beth nodded. "I didn't take as many naps today as yesterday and I think I'll have no problem sleeping tonight." She grinned. "Now I know why I don't take naps. Then I don't toss and turn during the night."

There was no way she was going to tell either Samuel or his daughter that the main reason she didn't sleep well was her dream, centered around the man standing not two feet from her. It wasn't every day she discovered she was in love. Even though he had taken off his wedding ring several days ago, that didn't mean he loved her. And even if he did, she wasn't looking for a ready-made family. She'd raised one already.

"Daddy, I want some warm milk." Allie scooted back onto the navy-and-tan couch. "I don't want to toss and turn."

He narrowed his gaze on his daughter. "You don't toss and turn. You sleep like a log."

Allie lifted her chin and crossed her arms. "But I might start tonight."

Beth chuckled. "She's got you there." She had to admit Allie was adorable, and so were Craig and Jane. Okay, she couldn't kid herself about his children. She cared about them, but enough to take on another family? Whoa! He hadn't asked her to, so why was she thinking about becoming a member of Samuel's family?

"No, this is a new stall tactic."

"You think?" Beth tried to suppress her laugh, but the exasperated look on Samuel's face made her giggle leak out.

"Eight-thirty is too early for someone my age to go to bed." Allie puffed out her chest. "Cindy isn't my age yet and she goes to bed at nine. I think I should be able to stay up at least as late as Cindy Blackburn."

Samuel squared his shoulders as if he were going to do battle. "I've got news for you, young lady—you are not Cindy Blackburn. It's still a school night and Allie Morgan goes to bed at eight-thirty." He checked his watch. "Which is right now."

"But, Daddy—"

He shook his head once. "No argument. We'll discuss your bedtime when it isn't your bedtime."

Allie pushed herself to her feet, her shoulders hunched over, a dejected look on her face. "Can we talk about it tomorrow?"

"That will depend on how fast you get ready for bed."

Allie ran from the room. The sound of her going up the stairs reminded Beth of a stampede of cattle she'd seen in a movie earlier that day while trying to do something when the children were at school and Samuel was at the church. She was afraid she drove Mae crazy with all her talk. Idleness wasn't her cup of tea.

"You've got the magic touch," Beth said, rising from the couch so Samuel didn't tower over her.

"No, you do. My kids stayed at the dining-room table long after we had eaten because of you. They enjoy your company." His look snared hers. "I enjoy your company. Are you sure you have to leave tomorrow?"

Chapter Twelve

"Yes, I've been here for four days. That's long enough." Beth knew she should move away from Samuel, but his look held her transfixed.

"What are your plans after that?"

The question that she had been avoiding since she had found out about having cancer hung between them. "I don't know," she finally answered, chilled by the uncertainty of her future. "I contacted the Christian Mission Institute and told them I couldn't take the job, but that's all I've done."

He stepped forward, taking her hand between his. "You haven't had much time to think about what you're going to do after you recover. I meant what are you going to do in the next few weeks?"

"Oh." The warmth of his hands cupping

hers flowed through her, taking with it any coldness his question had produced.

"Since school is out in three weeks, you won't be going back this year, and I know firsthand—" his mouth lifted in a lopsided grin "—how you like to be kept busy."

"I could help with the auction, and I can still tutor Jane until school is out."

"She'll appreciate that and I'm sure Jesse and Zoey will appreciate any help with the auction. But what are you going to do for yourself?"

"I—I…" Beth couldn't think of anything. She wanted to say it was because Samuel was so close and robbing her of any rational thought, which was partially true. But deep down she knew the reason she couldn't think of anything was that all her life she had lived for others. The trip to Brazil had been for her, and yet now that wasn't possible.

"That's what I was afraid of, Beth. You don't know how to plan things for yourself. Tell me one thing you would like to do when you feel up to it. Is there some place you would like to go that is within a few hours of here? What do you want to do?"

An idea popped into her mind, and she smiled. "Hot air ballooning."

"Done."

"What do you mean, done?"

"I'm giving you a month to get back on your feet physically, and then you and I have a date to go hot air ballooning."

"But I don't know of anyone in Sweetwater who has one."

"That isn't your problem. Leave everything to me. For once let someone take care of you." He tugged her toward the door. "I need to say good-night to Allie. Want to come?"

"Love to."

As she followed Samuel up to the second floor and his youngest daughter's bedroom, she realized how much she looked forward to saying good-night to Allie. She missed that routine with her siblings. She missed Holly. She missed her two brothers. Tears swelled her throat. Of late she seemed more emotional, and hoped that would settle down soon.

Several books were stacked on Allie's lap as she sat in her white canopy bed, waiting for her father. "I want you to read this tonight." She held up a big thick book. "No, I think I want to hear this one." She put the first story down and selected another one. "Will you read it to me, Beth?"

Beth glanced at Samuel, who nodded. "Sure. I loved *Black Beauty*."

"I'm gonna learn to ride like Crystal."

Alarm rang through Beth's mind when she thought of the riding accident that had led to Crystal's being in a wheelchair. Beth's protective instincts came to the fore. Then she peered at Allie's eager expression and remembered what it had been like when she'd been Allie's age and wanted to ride horses. She wasn't Allie's mother, and even if she was, she would need to learn to let go. That had been a hard lesson for her while raising her siblings. Even now she still felt responsible for them, still worried about them.

"Do you know how to ride a horse?"

The little girl's question pulled Beth back to the present. "I rode when I was a teenager. I haven't since then."

"Maybe you could take lessons with me."

Clearing her throat, Beth opened the book. "We'll see."

"That always means no when Daddy says that."

Beth peered at Samuel, who stood by the door watching them, his arms folded over his chest, his shoulder cushioned against the jamb. "But it doesn't mean no when I say it.

I'm just not sure of my plans once I get better. I don't want to make a promise I can't keep."

"Okay." Allie scooted over so that Beth could lean back against the headboard next to her.

Samuel couldn't take his eyes off Beth. Captivated, he observed her read to his daughter as though Allie was the most important person in Beth's life. Any lingering reservations about taking off his wedding ring were gone as he took in the picture of Beth and Allie sitting side by side, their heads bent together. His heartbeat sped up. He rubbed his sweaty palms up and down his arms.

He loved Beth Coleman. She would be a perfect mother for his children. She was good for him. She made him realize what was important in life: God, family and friends.

Then he remembered Beth's dream to travel, to serve the Lord in other parts of the world. How could he deny her that dream if he truly loved her?

A rough roar from the propane burner pierced the air, then quiet wrapped around Beth as she stared down at Sweetwater below the hot air balloon. A breeze cooled the warm June day, relieving the heat of summer. She saw her house, the church and Samuel's place, the lake with several boats on it. Jesse stood on her deck with Cindy next to her, waving at them. Beth returned the greeting as Nick came out to put his arm around his wife's shoulders and pull her close. Nate ran around the side of the house and up the stairs, joining the others.

A lump formed in Beth's throat. Jesse and Nick were so perfect for each other. Why couldn't she have found someone when she was younger? Her bout with cancer had only confirmed in her mind that she needed to do something for herself. Soon she should reapply to the Christian Mission Institute. If everything went well, in six weeks her doctor would release her, with a daily pill the only indication she'd had cancer.

The loud rushing sound cut into her thoughts as Samuel shot flames up to heat the air in the balloon. It rose above the lake, the wind stronger. The basket swayed. Beth gripped its rim to steady herself while Samuel came to stand beside her.

She slid her gaze to Samuel. "How did you arrange this?"

"With some help from Nick, who knew someone in Lexington. I told you I wanted to fulfill one of your dreams."

"You've been up in a balloon before?"

He nodded. "Quite a few times. I'm certified to fly one, so don't worry. You're safe with me."

"I'm discovering there's a lot I don't know about you."

"Isn't that what getting to know a person is all about, discovering those little things? I dated Ruth for three years and was married to her for thirteen, and she still was able to surprise me." He stepped back to hit the burner so the air in the balloon heated up.

When he returned to her side, Beth looked down at his hands clasping the railing in front of him and noticed that the area on his left finger where his wedding band used to be wasn't white anymore. In the six weeks since the surgery, she had started to dream something different. Samuel was always there to help her through any rough spots with the cancer treatment. He listened to her, especially when she felt depressed. He and his children had even helped her around the house and in her yard with chores when she had been overly tired. She wondered if, in his

mind, she was taking the place of Ruth, since
he had never had the chance to do those
things for his wife.

After firing the burner again, Samuel
stood back and studied her. "I hate to use
the cliché, but a penny for your thoughts.
You look so serious. This is supposed to be
for fun."

She pushed away the nagging doubt and
managed to smile. "I'm having fun. I just
started thinking about the past six weeks. I
shouldn't have."

"Why not?"

She gestured to her face. "Because of that
serious expression."

"I don't want you ever to feel you can't say
anything to me. I didn't like you thinking you
couldn't tell me about the cancer. I hope
we've gone beyond that."

She nodded, feeling closer to him in that
moment than she ever had. "Then I have a
question for you. For the past six weeks why
have you been there every time I needed
someone, sometimes when I didn't even
know it? Does it have anything to do with
Ruth and her fight against cancer?"

Samuel sucked in a deep breath, moving
back a step and almost absently hitting the

burner to keep the balloon in the air. "You don't pull any punches."

"Not anymore. You wanted to know what I was thinking."

He cocked his head to the side and looked beyond her. When he reestablished eye contact with her, he said, "I won't lie to you. Yes, it has something to do with Ruth."

Her heart skipped a beat, then began to pound, its sound thundering in her ears.

"And no, it doesn't have anything really to do with her. I don't think I can separate it so cleanly. What happened to Ruth has affected me and shaped me into the man I am today."

Vaguely Beth was aware of the silence, the fresh summer smells carried on the breeze, the warmth of the sun, but all her senses were focused on the man before her.

He covered the small space between them and drew her up against him. "I did all those things because I love you, Beth. You are a caring, compassionate woman who my children adore, who I adore."

His declaration stole her voice, her thoughts and her breath. When they all returned in a rush, tears filled her eyes and made his image blurry. "I love you, too, Samuel."

He bent forward and brushed his lips across hers before settling his mouth over hers and winding his arms around her. His kiss rocked her to her soul. Never in her life had she been kissed as though she was the most special woman in the world. Beautiful. Cherished. Loved.

She laid her head against the cushion of his shoulder, feeling the rise and fall of his chest, hearing his heartbeat beneath the thin knit of his shirt. "Where do we go from here?"

He stroked her back, his touch soft, comforting. "I don't know. I never expected to fall in love again. To tell you the truth, I didn't want to fall in love again. I never want to experience the pain and devastation that occurred after Ruth died."

She leaned back and looked into his dark eyes, shining with the love he had expressed only a moment before. But within she also saw uncertainty. "I think we take it slow and easy and see where it leads us. I'd given up on love and moved on with plans that didn't include it. Then I got cancer and things changed again."

He cupped her cheek. "I know. We never know what's really around the next corner." Rubbing his thumb across her lips, he smiled at her, but there was a sadness in the slight upturn of his mouth.

When he left her alone at the railing while he brought the hot air balloon safely to the ground, Beth closed her eyes for a few minutes, trying to assimilate what had just happened between them. Her mind felt overloaded, and she couldn't quite figure out what to do. She loved him. She loved his children. But was she prepared to take on a ready-made family…again? Would she be totally happy and content giving up on her dream? Was it fair to put Samuel in the position of going through with her what happened to his first wife? Her prognosis was good, but there was a chance the cancer could return. Massaging the sides of her temples, she realized she didn't have an answer.

Beth sat on a red plaid blanket under a large oak tree and watched the young children enjoying the church playground. Allie was swinging next to Cindy, while Sean and Nate were climbing on the jungle gym. Off to the side of the playground a group of teenagers were in the middle of a fierce volleyball game. Jane leaped into the air and smashed the ball across the net at her brother's feet, scoring a point for her team. Several of the members gave her a high five as Jane's boyfriend readied himself to serve again.

Another Fourth of July picnic and auction. But this time it was different because of Samuel and his family.

"Jane's a changed girl because of you, Beth."

She slanted a look at Zoey, who settled cross-legged on the blanket across from her. "She wanted to change or she wouldn't have, no matter what I did."

"Don't sell yourself short. You were there to help her when she needed it. You had faith in her and her ability. You're good at doing that, especially for the kids at school. They all missed you at the end of the year."

"I missed them."

Beth recalled the party her classes had thrown for her the day after school was out for the summer. Samuel had driven her to school to turn in her grades. When she'd gone to her room to input them into the computer, she had been surprised by many of her students.

"What have you decided to do come August?" Zoey smoothed the blanket in front of her, picking up a leaf and tossing it away.

"I don't know. I don't understand why I can't make a decision."

Zoey stared at Samuel talking to a group of parishioners near the tables laden with food. "I understand why you can't. Two opposing dreams are colliding. I know you've wanted to do mission work for years and were just waiting until your siblings grew up."

"Samuel told me last week that he loves me." Beth found him in the crowd, his hands gesturing as they often did when he talked. She smiled. "He's such a good man."

"You don't have to sell me on that. He's done an excellent job taking over the ministry. Somewhere in what you're saying to me I hear a 'but.'"

"I don't know if I can raise a family all over again." Beth glanced at her friend. "I don't know if he isn't confusing me with his wife, possibly subconsciously thinking he has a second chance concerning the cancer. He was devastated when he couldn't help Ruth." She motioned in Samuel's direction. "Have you taken a good look at him? He's handsome while I am…" She let her sentence trail off into the noise around them.

"What? Plain? Are you fishing for compliments, Beth Coleman?"

Beth straightened. "No."

"Well, I'm going to give them to you anyway. You *are* beautiful. I bet he's told you that, too, hasn't he?"

Beth nodded.

"Especially lately. There's a glow about you—from a look in your eyes to the way your whole face lights up, especially when Samuel is near. And you've finally gotten rid of your drab clothes." Zoey pointed toward Beth's red capri pants and red, white and blue T-shirt. "I doubt he's mixed you up with his dead wife. But as for the other doubt you have, only you can decide if taking on three more children is what you want. It's a serious, important decision and I don't envy you that. From the way his children are around you, they wouldn't mind if you did."

"We do get along, but being their mother would be different. I would be responsible for them 24/7."

"Has he asked you to marry him?"

Beth again searched out Samuel in the crowd. "Not in so many words, but we have skirted the issue several times in the past few days. Maybe I'm jumping the gun here."

Zoey shook her head. "I don't think so.

"And the proceeds go to a worthy cause."

"Are you excited about the new prison ministry program?"

"You bet. It'll be a challenge, but then I thrive on challenges."

"How's Tom doing?"

"Not good. When he allows me to see him, he refuses to talk about Tanya, Crystal or Sweetwater. It's as if he's cut out that part of his life."

"Maybe that's the only way he can survive prison."

A frown slashed across Samuel's features. "But he won't be in prison forever. His daughter needs her father."

"I know. It's hard when a father abandons his child."

His attention swerved to Beth. "You never talk about your own father."

"He walked out on us before Daniel was born, so what's left to say? He didn't want the responsibility of raising another child. I don't know where he is. It's as though he has vanished from our lives."

"When your mother died, did you try to find him?"

She shook her head. "I won't force myself on anyone."

"But Daniel was a baby."

"And *my* responsibility."

"You were all alone with three children."

"Ethan was only a few years younger than me, and my father's uncle helped from time to time. My great-uncle died a couple of years back and some distant relative took over his farm. That's all the family I have."

His dark gaze bored into her. "You have me and my family. I love you and when you are ready, I want to marry you."

Her breath caught in her throat. "Is that a proposal?"

His whole face shone with a smile that reached deep into his eyes. "Yes, it is. I hadn't really planned to ask at the picnic, but I won't take the words back."

"I—" She clamped her mouth shut, not sure what to say.

He touched her lips with his finger. "Don't answer right now. I know you love me, but marriage is much more than that. I want a family with you, a baby. We'll talk—"

"Daddy." Allie threw herself at her father. "It's time to eat. C'mon!" She pulled back and tugged on Samuel's hand to get him to stand.

Hovering over Beth, Samuel captured her

gaze and said, "We'll talk later when it's less public. Right now we'd better eat before all the good food is gone."

The promise in his words sent a thrill through Beth. Rising, she followed the pair toward the tables lined with all types of salads, side dishes and desserts. As she piled food onto her paper plate, all she could think about was Samuel's proposal. Marriage. A family. A baby. The decision wasn't a simple yes or no. She hadn't told him yet about the offer she'd received yesterday from the Christian Mission Institute.

Samuel said goodbye to the last members of the cleanup crew as they filed out of the rec hall. When he turned back toward the table where Beth sat, adding up the purchases, he saw Zoey and Jesse join her. Aunt Mae had taken his children home, and he intended to have some quiet time with Beth just as soon as her friends left.

The whole afternoon his thoughts had been filled with his proposal to Beth. He wasn't even sure he had been too coherent when talking with others. At one point, Joshua had had to ask a question twice before he answered.

The one overriding conclusion he'd come to as the afternoon had progressed was that Beth was the right woman for him and his family. But he wasn't sure he and his family were right for her. How could he ask her to start her life over, raising a whole new family? And he had probably really frightened her when he had blurted out that he wanted a baby with her. How could he ask her to give up a dream of traveling and doing God's work? He shouldn't have been so impulsive and asked her to marry him without thinking of her needs. He didn't want her to feel obligated to marry him because she loved him and he loved her. He'd seen firsthand as a minister that wasn't always enough.

With a deep sigh he strode toward Beth, praying to God to show him the way.

"I'm so glad that the auction is over and was a success. See these." Jesse held up her hands. "I've bitten off all my fingernails. They are stubs."

"You're a natural organizer, Jesse. We pulled in more money this year than any in the past." Beth finished the tally of the proceeds and gave the sheet to her friend.

Jesse looked at it, then smiled. "This is wonderful." She passed it to Samuel. "You're

the reason this was such a success this year,
Beth. Zoey and I couldn't have done it without your guidance and notes. You've built the
auction up until now practically the whole
town turns out."

Beth laughed. "Hardly. But it was nice to
see every space filled with people bidding."

"Samuel, I hope I can persuade you to
build another dollhouse. My daughter was
very disappointed I didn't get it." Zoey gathered up the sale receipts and checks and
placed them in a metal box.

"You're about the fifth person who has
asked me that today."

Jesse winced. "Sorry, Zoey. Cindy fell in
love with the dollhouse."

"That's okay. Nick made a hefty donation
to our outreach program for that dollhouse
and that's the most important thing. Remember last year when he bought your
doll?"

Jesse got a dreamy look on her face. "Yes.
Wasn't that sweet of him? And he told me
right after the auction today that he was
whisking me away to a secluded island in the
Caribbean for a week of R and R. No kids,
just the two of us."

"That's great!" Beth exclaimed. "A beach,

sun and sand. That sounds wonderful after all the time you've put in with the auction."

"After our vacation I'm thinking of taking the kids with us on Nick's business trip to Europe. I may be away for most of July."

Samuel watched the wistful expression appear in Beth's eyes. Serving in the army as a chaplain, he'd done what Beth wanted to do. How could he stand in her way? Not if he truly loved her.

Zoey rose, the metal box in hand. "I don't know about you all, but I'm tired. It's been a long day and I still have to deposit the money in the bank."

"I need to leave, too. I have bags to pack and plans to make." Jesse grabbed the rest of the paperwork and glanced around. "Looks like the cleanup crew did a great job. See you."

When Zoey and Jesse left, Samuel faced Beth, taking her hand. "Do you feel up to a walk in the garden?"

She nodded, the usual sparkle in her eyes gone.

"Are you sure you're not too tired?" Samuel asked.

"No, I'm fine. I was just thinking."

Samuel headed outside with Beth next to him. "About Jesse's trip?"

"That and something I need to tell you."

"That sounds ominous."

She shrugged. "I haven't had a chance to tell you I got a letter from the Christian Mission Institute."

Samuel led Beth to the path that took them to the pond in the garden. "What did they have to say?" The beating of his heart slowed.

She took a seat on the bench, leaving him room next to her if he wanted to sit. "They have a temporary position for me at another mission near Belém in Brazil. It could work itself into a permanent position if I want, but right now a worker needs to come back to the United States for personal reasons at the beginning of August."

His chest tightened. He inhaled a deep breath, but couldn't fill his lungs.

"I'm not sure what I should do."

Again he tried to draw air into his lungs, but the band about his chest constricted his efforts. He turned away as though the goldfish in the pond were the most fascinating creatures he'd seen. Closing his eyes, he quickly asked for strength to do what was right for Beth.

When he looked back at her and saw her

worry and concern, he forced a smile and said, "You have to take the position."

"But what about us? Your proposal?"

Chapter Thirteen

Samuel kept his distance, his smile gone. "You have to do this. If you don't, you'll always wonder and regret the wasted opportunity."

Her teeth dug into her bottom lip. Had something changed in the few hours since his proposal? Beth realized she wasn't very good at knowing the ins and outs of a relationship, since she'd had so few of them over the years. Why wasn't he demanding she stay and marry him?

She rose on shaky legs. "I could be gone a long time."

"I know."

She started toward the parking lot. "Then I'll call them immediately and tell them yes."

Halfway down the stone path Samuel stopped her with a hand on her arm. "Beth—"

She shook off his hand and hurried forward. Tears misted her eyes, making it difficult to see the path.

"Beth."

The plea in his voice stopped her. But she didn't turn around.

"I will be here when you are ready to get married, but I've seen people give up their dreams for another. It can build a wall between two people that is impossible to scale. When you walk down the aisle, I want it to be for all the right reasons."

Slowly she faced him. "Then I'll go."

"Why do you have to go?" Allie asked with a pout.

Beth finished zipping up her suitcase, then placed it next to her bed before answering, "They're counting on me to be there."

"But I want you here." Allie stomped her foot and pointed to the floor. "I might need someone to help me when school starts at the end of the month. I'm going into the third grade, you know."

"Your dad can help, and so can Jane."

Tears glistened in Allie's eyes. "It's not the same."

Beth sank onto the bed and motioned for

Allie to come to her. She wrapped her arms around the child. "You can write me and if there's a computer at the mission, I can e-mail you, maybe even send you some pictures. I'm taking my digital camera."

"But you won't be here."

It was harder for her to leave than Beth had ever imagined, and yet she had committed herself to going to the mission and she would. Samuel was right. She needed to do this for herself. But holding Allie and having to tell her goodbye ripped at her heart.

"We'll see each other again," Beth finally whispered.

Allie pulled back. "When?"

"I'm not sure how long I'll be staying. I'm filling in for someone taking a leave, then I may stay."

"Why?"

"Because God wants me to."

"Why can't God want you to be here with us? God needs workers here, too. Others can go to the mission. Why does it have to be you?"

Beth brushed the child's hair back from her face. "I promised them I would come."

Tears streamed down her cheeks. "Do you promise to come home?"

Beth spied Samuel in the doorway, sadness

in his eyes, and her heart broke into two pieces. Why had she agreed to go when she had him? Why was she so afraid to make a total commitment to his family?

Beth looked back at the little girl. "Yes, I promise to come home."

Allie threw herself at Beth and kissed her on the cheek. "Don't stay away long, please."

"Allie, I need to drive Beth to the airport. We don't want her to miss her plane."

Allie spun around. "Yes, I do, Daddy."

"Come on. The rest of the family is in the foyer waiting, Allie. Let Beth finish getting her things together."

Sighing, Allie trudged toward the door, her shoulders hunched. As she disappeared into the hallway, Beth rose.

"I'm sorry about that." Samuel came into her bedroom.

"That's okay. I knew she wasn't happy with me."

"I tried to explain to her last night, but I guess I wasn't successful." He pulled up the handle on the suitcase so he could roll it toward the door.

"I'm sorry."

He halted and turned back to her. "About what?"

"About causing Allie any pain, about us."

Letting go of the suitcase, he strode the few feet to her and clasped her upper arms. "You have nothing to be sorry for. You have to do this. That doesn't mean we are happy about it, but we will live through it. If you decide working at the mission is what you need to do, then I will learn to accept that decision." He pulled her to him. "I love you. I want what's best for you."

His words comforted and yet pained her at the same time. She laid her head against his heart, needing to hear its steady, strong beat, so much like the man.

"Right now my family needs Sweetwater and what it can offer them. You need the mission near Belém. We'll be here when you want to come home." He leaned back and framed her face, his intense gaze on her.

When he lowered his head and covered her mouth with his, she melted against him and poured all her love into the kiss. The memory of it would have to last her a long time. Savoring the taste of him on her lips, she finally pulled away.

"I only have a few things to gather for the plane ride. I'll be out in a minute."

Watching him leave with her big suitcase,

Beth managed to keep herself together until he was gone. Then the tears came, rolling down her face unchecked.

God, why isn't life as easy as Allie thinks it is?

The rain fell in gray sheets outside the window at the mission. Beth stared at the line of trees marking the edge of the clearing where the jungle began. Eight weeks had slipped by. She loved working in the school with the small children, and if she cared to, the director wanted her to stay on permanently.

But every day for the past eight weeks she had missed Samuel and his children. She felt good about the work she was doing for the Lord, but there was an emptiness inside her she couldn't fill with her prayers.

God needs workers here, too.

Beth remembered Allie's plea to her that last day in Sweetwater. She hadn't been able to get the child's words out of her mind. She didn't have to go thousands of miles from home to do God's work. There was a need in Sweetwater, as there was any place.

Was she ready for a family? Because Samuel came with one. In fact, he wanted more children. After working with the young children at the mission she knew she wanted to be a mother in every sense of the word, from giving birth to raising the child, as she had her siblings.

She had a lot of love inside her—love she wanted to give to Samuel and his children. She needed to go home, and hoped that Samuel still wanted her as his wife, since he hadn't mentioned it in his e-mails.

Beth rose from the desk and walked to the open window, listening to the steady downpour. Through the gray she caught sight of some orchids growing in a tree. Such beauty here. Raw. Untamed. She was glad she had experienced this, but without Samuel it didn't mean much. He defined her life, made her complete, and it had taken coming to Brazil for her to realize that fully.

The sound of children's feet alerted her to the beginning of class. She turned from the window and greeted her pupils as they entered the classroom.

"I thought I would find you here, Dad." Jane slipped into the pew next to Samuel at the front of the church.

He glanced at his watch. "School's out already?"

Jane grinned. "Has been for an hour."

"How was it today? Any problems?"

"Don't worry, Dad. I'll get help if I need it from whoever I need to. Beth taught me that, to ask for help."

"Beth taught us all something."

"What did she teach you?"

He sighed. "To trust in the Lord. To turn to Him when things are hard to deal with."

"Is that why you come in here every day before coming home?"

He chuckled. "I work here."

"It's more than that, Dad."

"True. Yes, I like to talk with God before going home. This place—" he scanned the sanctuary "—is comforting."

"It reminds you of Beth?"

He nodded. "She was so much a part of this church."

"Everyone misses her. Do you think she misses us?"

"In her e-mails she says she does."

"Then why doesn't she come home?"

"She will if it's meant to be."

"How can you sit there and calmly say that?"

He turned to face his daughter. "Because I have faith that the Lord will do what is best for all of us."

"Beth is best for us."

He took his oldest daughter's hand between his. "I hope He sees it that way. I hope she does. That's all I can do, hon. Hope and pray."

Jane rose. "I will, too. Maybe it will be enough."

As his daughter started for the door, it opened. Jane gasped and hurried forward. Not able to see who it was, Samuel pushed to his feet and turned toward the back. Jane threw her arms around the person still partially hidden, but Samuel knew who it was.

He rushed down the aisle as Jane pulled Beth into full view. He stopped, taking in the sight of the woman he loved. From her expression he knew she had come home for good.

"I'm leaving," Jane said, but her words sounded so far away.

All Samuel could see was Beth's beautiful smiling face that glowed with a promise of love. She took a step toward him. He moved forward. Then somehow they were in each other's arms.

He kissed her on the forehead, the cheek, then the mouth. "Why didn't you let me know you were coming? I could have picked you up at the airport."

"I wanted to surprise you, and it looks like I did. I took a chance you were still at the church. When I couldn't find you in your office, I thought you might be in here."

"You did?"

"Call it a hunch. It was good to see Jane. Is she really doing all right in school? She wrote me she was."

"The first nine weeks will be over soon and she has good grades so far, but she works hard for them."

"How are Allie and Craig?"

"There isn't a day Allie doesn't ask about you. And Craig is on a football team. It's his whole life right now."

"I can't wait to see them."

He cupped her face, his fingers delving into her curls. "Will you marry me?"

"Why do you think I came back?"

"I'll take that as a yes."

"Yes, that's a yes. For years I thought I wanted the single life, not having to be responsible for anyone but me. I was wrong. I missed not having a family. It took going thousands of miles away to finally realize that, but I want children and a husband. I want my own family. I want you and the kids."

"No more traveling?"

She smiled. "I didn't say that. I've decided to organize mission trips for our youth every summer. It's something we have talked about doing but haven't done yet. Now is the time. Our outreach program is expanding, especially with the success of events like the auction."

"You are never going to change. Already home less than an hour and you have a new job."

"Speaking of a job, I'm going to substitute for the remainder of the school year. One of the teachers in the English department is going on maternity leave in a few weeks and I'm going to take over her classes until the end of the semester."

"It doesn't bother you not to have your own classes?"

"No, because I think I'll be busy making plans for my wedding."

"Not to mention the mission trip for next summer."

She snuggled closer. "You know I can't stay idle."

"Have you ever thought of having your own child?"

"Ever since I met you, many times," she

said with a laugh. "But I can't wait too long. I'm pushing forty."

Samuel wound his arm about her shoulders and headed for the door. "Then we need to get married soon."

Out in the foyer of the church the front door burst open and in raced Allie and Craig. Both practically tackled Beth in their enthusiasm to greet her.

"Hold it, you two. Let her breathe," Samuel said, watching his family show their love as though Beth had always been their mother.

"Jane told us you were back." Allie enclosed her arms about Beth's waist and pressed her head to her chest.

"I made a promise to a young lady that I had to keep."

Allie bent back to look up into Beth's face. "I knew something was up when you didn't answer my latest e-mail right away."

"Why don't you two go let Aunt Mae know there will be one more for dinner?"

Allie and Craig hurried toward the house.

"When I see you and your family, I can't imagine why I thought I needed to go to Brazil in the first place."

"What's ten weeks, three days—" he

checked his watch "—eight hours and twenty-four minutes in the grand scheme of things?"

"An eternity when you are away from the one you love."

Epilogue

"Look, that's Jane!" Allie pointed toward
the stage in the high school auditorium.

Beth's chest swelled as she watched Jane
walk to the superintendent of Sweetwater
schools and shake his hand, then take her
high school diploma from the principal. The
past few years hadn't been easy for Jane, but
she had done it and with a good grade point
average. She would be heading to the Uni-
versity of Kentucky in the fall.

Tears clogged Beth's throat as she thought
of Jane telling her that she wanted to be a
teacher and help students as Beth had.

Samuel laid his hand on her arm, pulling
her attention toward her husband.

"Jane owes you a lot."

"Samuel, I owe her a lot. She has given me so much."

"Mama, eat."

Her sixteen-month-old son wiggled out of Aunt Mae's arms and climbed over his father to get to Beth's lap. She rummaged in her large purse and found a plastic bag of cereal for Garrett. He plunged his chubby fingers inside and stuffed some of the round O's into his mouth.

Samuel leaned close to her ear and whispered, "Will you be okay when Jane leaves home?"

"No, but I'll deal with it. Besides, I'm going to be extra busy next year."

"Have you decided to go back to teaching?"

She shook her head. "No, we're having another baby."

Samuel pulled back, his dark eyes round. "We are?"

"Yes, around the middle of January."

He slipped his arm around her. "Beth Morgan, I love you."

* * * * *

Look for Zoey's story, only from
Margaret Daley
and Steeple Hill Love Inspired!

Dear Reader,

I hope you enjoyed Beth and Samuel's story in *Light in the Storm*. I am a high school teacher who has worked with students with learning disabilities. It is important to convey to them that they have strengths as well as weaknesses. Sometimes we dwell on our weaknesses and our self-esteem suffers for it. Yes, we need to be aware of what we need to work on, but no one is perfect. Jane needed to learn that in this story, as did Beth and Samuel.

Another aspect of my story was Beth's battle with breast cancer. With it being one of the common forms of cancer for women, I wanted to stress the importance of early detection. One way is monthly self-examination. There is a Buddy Check program that advocates a woman forming a partnership with a friend or family member; each reminds the other to self-check monthly.

I love hearing from my readers. You can contact me at P.O. Box 2074, Tulsa, OK 74101, or visit my Web site at www.margaretdaley.com.

Best wishes,

Margaret Daley

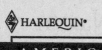
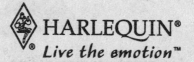